Irene!
Thank you f
the support.
It was wonderful
meeting you!

UNEXPECTED SURPRISES

Janet A. Mota

A special thank you to my family for all the support. I love you all so much.

Another special thank you to Vanessa Archbold and Kimberly Brown for reading an advanced copy and giving me your honest opinions on the book. You ladies rock!!

Prologue

Five Years Earlier

I open my eyes and look around. How did I get here? I look down and see the two bandages on my left arm. I lift the sheet and see two more large bandages on my left leg. A sharp pain shoots through my abdomen but my hospital gown covers my stomach. I can't see anything. I lay my head back again and rub my forehead. My head hurts. My whole body aches. What in the world happened?

A nurse walks into the room and looks at me. She smiles a gentle smile and starts to question me.

"How are you feeling?" She asks.

"My head hurts, and my body feels like I took a pounding," I respond.

She nods. "Can you tell me your name?" The nurse checks the machines hooked up to me. For some reason, she's avoiding eye contact and it bothers me.

"Katarina Rodrigues."

"Great. Your vitals look good. I'm going to call the doctor. My name is Caroline." She leans over me and points out a red button on the side of my bed. "Push this button whenever you need me."

"Thank you," I say, and she leaves the room. It wasn't a warm exchange and suddenly uneasy.

I close my eyes again. *Why am I here? How did I get all these bandages?* My mind is spinning, and I can't get a clear picture until a sudden vision appears so clearly.

I bring my hand to my mouth and tears instantly fall from my eyes. I'm seeing the wreckage. My husband and parents are covered in blood and unresponsive. My daughter and son are in the same condition. I pull my daughter out of her booster seat and lay her on the ground. I run around to the other side of the car. I unbuckle my son from his car seat and bring him over to lie next to his sister. I kneel between them and call out their names. Nothing happens. I yell for my husband, my mom, and my dad. No response. Suddenly, I'm being pulled to my feet and away from my children and the world goes black.

My heart's beating so hard it might jump out of my chest. Panic rushes me and I can't breathe. I sit up and start pressing the nurse's call button. *I need to get out of here. I need to find them. My poor babies must be so scared.* I'm starting to get out of bed when the nurse comes rushing in.

"What are you doing?" She gasps and rushes over to me.

"I need to get to my family," I yell.

The nurse bends down and lifts my legs to tuck them back under the sheet but I fight her and pull my legs out again.

"Stop!" I shout. "I need to get to my family! I'm fine! I don't need to be here! My babies need me!"

The nurse takes a step back and looks me in the eye. "You need to get back into bed until the doctor sees you. You hit your head hard, and you can't put too much pressure on your leg."

"How long will that take? I need to get to my family. They're all probably scared and confused. I need to be with them!" I yell. At this point, I just don't care how out of control I'm acting. She's keeping me from my world.

A male figure in a white lab coat and black dress pants walks into the room and smiles at me. He gives the nurse a nod. The nurse takes a step back and the man approaches me. He extends his hand toward me. I stare at him and don't take his hand. I know I'm being rude, but I need to get to my family.

"Hi, Katarina. I'm Dr. Andrews. I've been treating you since you were brought in."

"I need to get to my family," I tell him sternly.

"Unfortunately, there's no easy way to say this, so I'm just going to say it." He looks at me. He has such caring eyes, and I can see the sadness in them. "I'm sorry but your family didn't make it."

My legs give out and I drop to the floor. The nurse and the doctor are next to me in an instant. I can't think. I can't breathe. I start to hyperventilate. The doctor and nurse lift me and place me back into the bed. Tears fall from my eyes as they tuck me into the bed and adjust the monitors. The doctor puts an oxygen mask on my mouth and nose. "Deep breaths. In and out slowly."

The doctor speaks again, "I'm so sorry, Mrs. Rodrigues. I wish I didn't have to tell you that."

I cry. The doctor goes on to explain my injuries, but I don't hear him. I'm completely numb to him and everyone around me. My family is gone. Why? How? I don't understand.

Chapter 1

The Present

Five Years Later

After the last five years, I decided to come to Portugal for a getaway of sorts. Why Portugal? My parents are from this beautiful country, and it just made sense I would come to the place I vacationed as a child. Portugal means so much to me and it's time for me to reconnect with society. I'm hoping it will help me deal with losing my family. I can't seem to move on. I'm stuck in this holding pattern and can't find my way out. It still hurts so much. I still see the accident in my dreams. Every night I'm haunted by nightmares. Saying goodbye to them was completely unreal and pure hell.

I step off the plane, take a deep breath, continue down the stairs and walk the tarmac to the entrance of the airport. I get through customs and baggage claim quickly. For the past five years, I've just wandered around. I quit my job and decided to write novels to cope with the voices in my head. Two months after quitting my job, I wrote my first book and submitted it to a publishing company on a whim. The publishing company loved the book but said I needed to hire an agent to move on. After looking into some recommendations, I hired one. Now, I have three books published and working on a fourth. All my writings have included some type of death. I pour every feeling I carry into my books.

It's the anniversary of my family's death and I can't focus on anything. I need a change in the environment. Maybe it'll get my creative juices flowing again. The death of my family has put me into severe depression. I didn't want to leave my house or do anything. I wrote and only left the house for groceries. I wouldn't fix my hair or get new clothes. I wore the same three pairs of worn jeans and four sweatshirts. Why bother? My whole family was gone in a matter of minutes. Burying my children, husband, and parents on the same day was the worst thing I've ever had to do. I wouldn't wish it on anyone. After two years of solitude, I just couldn't take it anymore. I wanted to end my life.

One night, I walked into the bathroom and turned on the water in the shower. I undressed and got in. I picked up my razor, released the blade, and took it to my wrist. As I started cutting, I realized doing this wouldn't solve anything. I was kept alive for a reason, and I wouldn't take the cowardly way out. I slumped down onto the shower floor and cried. I don't know how much time passed. I didn't realize the water ran cold. When I calmed myself, I noticed the blood. I turned off the shower and dried off. I carefully wrapped the wounds with a towel to stop the bleeding. I bandaged myself and never told a soul what I tried to do. I have an ugly scar on my wrist to remind me of what I almost did every single day.

I hail a cab and fish the address from my purse. I hand the driver the address and we're off. I take in the sites and I'm glad I chose to come here. I'll be staying at my uncle's apartment at the beach. I called Uncle Manny and asked him to rent me the apartment. He was so happy I finally decided to get away for a little while. He mailed me the keys and told me to stay as long as I needed. They're coming for a wedding next month but are staying at a nearby hotel because they're only coming for a few days. I thanked him and was truly grateful the apartment was available to me. That apartment holds special memories.

The cab driver pulls in front of a beige building with beautiful blue tile and white railings on the balconies. The building has about ten floors and the apartment I'll be staying in is on the ninth. I pay the driver and jump out. The bags are already waiting for me on the curb. There aren't any elevators and I proceed up the stairs with my bags. When I finally reach the apartment, I pull the keys from my pocket and unlock the door. I walk in and drop my bags by the door. The apartment smells a little musty, so I open the French doors leading out to the balcony. Fresh air immediately engulfs me, and I close my eyes and take it in. I step out onto the balcony and take in the view. It's spectacular. The beach is directly in front of me, and I can see the shops and cafes on my left. I know I'll enjoy my time here. I need this escape. Maybe I can finally start to move on. My family would've wanted that. Living as a shut-in is not healthy and I know it needs to stop. I need some closure, something that will start helping me heal.

I take in the view for a moment longer then go back inside. It's time to unpack. I grab my bags and head into the first bedroom on the right, just past the bathroom. Just off the kitchen is an open area which is the living room/dining room. It has a sofa and a loveseat with a small TV in the corner. In the dining room space, there's a wood table with six chairs. Next to the dining room is a small bathroom with a tiny shower. There are two more bedrooms to the left of what's going to be my bedroom. The apartment is way more than I need but it's on the beach. I grab a nearby pad and pen and jot down a grocery list. Time to head out to get some food. For the first time in a very long time, I'm looking forward to doing the task.

****

The street along the beachfront is filled with shops and cafés. At the corner is a bakery. I walk a little further and pass a pharmacy, some clothing shops, and a shoe store. As I walk, my eyes don't leave the beach. It's deserted. It's January, so the tourists haven't arrived yet. The beach looks so beautiful. I stop and take in the sight. The water's choppy and looks angry. It's so cold. I wrap my jacket around me, breathe in the salty air, and continue walking. At the end of the block is a small grocery store. I open the door and the bell above the door chimes. The older man behind the counter looks up and smiles. I nod and grab a basket.

Twenty minutes later, I'm headed back to the apartment. I look toward the ocean again. *Note to self-I need to bring my laptop out here to see if I can get out of this rut I'm in.* The noise of the waves lapping on the shore angrily is relaxing. I could stare at the water for hours. *Maybe tonight I'll come for a cup of coffee and watch the water.* I reach my building, unlock the door, and head up the stairs.

A minute later, I'm walking through the door and into the kitchen. I unpack all the groceries. I start a pot of coffee and go into the dining room to set up my laptop on the table. Once it's all set up to my liking, I walk back into the kitchen and prepare a cup of coffee. I walk to the French doors, open them, and walk out onto the balcony. I sit down on one of the two chairs and bring my legs up. I wrap my arms around my knees and watch the waves lap the shore. I refuse to let my thoughts wander and I stare at the beauty of nature before me. I'm happy with the decision I made. I have a good feeling about coming here.

Chapter 2

Kat

I stay on the balcony for hours. I didn't have dinner and I'm not hungry. I check my watch. Eight o'clock. It's time to go back inside. I close the doors and turn off the kitchen light. I walk into my bedroom, turn on the bedside lamp, and open the closet. I grab my toiletries case and take it into the bathroom. I brush my teeth and get myself ready for bed. I throw on my pajamas. They're so old but extremely comfortable. I reach into my handbag and pull out the romance novel I started on the plane. I get into bed and begin to read.

An hour later, I place the marker in the book and close it. I stretch. I'm tired, but I know I'm not going to get any sleep; if I do, the nightmares will take over. I need to try anyway. I place the book on the bedside table and click off the light. I stare at the ceiling. The night is cold, so the blanket over me feels good. I start to drift off when I hear shuffling at the front door. I sit up and listen. The shuffling gets louder. I quickly jump out of bed and run into the kitchen. I grab a frying pan, which is hanging near the stove. It happens to be the first thing I see. I stand next to the door, holding the pan in both hands above my head. The lock clicks and the door opens.

"Stop!" I yell.

The figure stops in the doorway.

"Don't move or I'll hit you," I say sternly.

"Who are you and why are you here?" A thick voice booms. This guy is huge. I can see his profile in the darkness. He can kill me, and I'm ready to stand off with a frying pan. *Really?!*

"I should be asking you that question." I'm still holding the frying pan above my head and my heart is booming in my ears. Th this guy wants to, he could've overpowered me by now.

"My name is Reinaldo Vaz. My uncle owns this place and he's letting me stay here for a couple of weeks," he says.

"What?!" I respond and drop my hands. I reach over and click on the light.

There he stands, facing me. I can't believe my eyes. He looks gorgeous. Tall, dark, and so freaking handsome. Those hazel eyes staring at me make my stomach do flips. He looks like he just jumped out of a magazine cover. He's wearing jeans, a black shirt, and a leather jacket. He stands just over six feet tall with a massive build. After all these years, he still makes my heart skip a beat. Damn man gets better with age. What the hell?

"Kat." He says, and we just stand there looking at each other. He breaks his gaze and looks down at my hands. "Nice weapon." He smirks.

"It would've been effective," I say and shrug.

"You look great." He's smiling at me. I don't smile back. I just stare at him. I still can't believe he's standing right in front of me.

"Liar," I say. "But thanks."

I step into the kitchen and hang the frying pan where it was. Rey pulls his bags from the hallway into the apartment, closes the door, and follows me into the kitchen.

"Would you like something to drink? Coffee? I can make a pot." I ask him. He smiles at me, nods, and pulls out a chair. He removes his jacket and hangs it on the back of the chair. The muscles in his arms scream out from under his shirt. I'm trying not to stare but I'm pretty sure I just embarrassed myself. *Why am I acting like this? Pull yourself together. This isn't high school.*

"I would love some. Thanks." He says, sitting down and stretching his long legs out in front of him. He looks up at me. "I'm sorry I scared you. Uncle Manny didn't tell me you would be here. I thought it would be empty."

"It's okay. I have no idea why he didn't tell you I was staying here. I know you wouldn't have come if you knew I was staying here, especially in the middle of the night." I turn the coffee pot on and look at him. I lean against the counter and cross my arms in front of my chest. "I'm renting this place from him for the next three months. I got here this afternoon. When did you make plans with Uncle Manny?"

"About two months ago. I found out I was going to have a leave from service and decided to come to my cousin's wedding. They told me they would be here. I figured I would come to the wedding and see them too. I haven't been here since I was a kid and thought it would be fun." He shrugs. "Why? When did you make plans with our uncle?"

"I made plans with him about five months ago. I've had severe writer's block and I have to have a new book written in the next couple of months. I decided to come here. I haven't been back here since I was a kid, too. I thought a change of pace would be good for me and maybe get my creative juices flowing." I tell him, pondering why Uncle Manny didn't say anything to either of us.

"Good plan. I hope it works." He looks around the small space. "Well, since you got here first you get to stay here. I'll find a hotel or someplace else to stay. I'll call Uncle Manny in the morning and let him know."

I turn and get two coffee mugs from the cupboard. "There's no need to go to a hotel. I can share it. This apartment is big enough for both of us." I pour the coffee and turn to him. "How do you take your coffee?" *What am I doing? Did I just ask him to stay here with me?*

"Just black," he says. "Kat, are you sure? I don't want to get in your way. You made plans to stay here before I did. It's only fair you stay here."

I hand him his coffee and sit across from him. "It's fine. You won't get in my way." I take a sip and look up at him. He's watching every move I make. My heart kicks up again. Butterflies take flight in my stomach. *What is with this reaction?* I feel like he can see right through me, and it makes me nervous. I start fidgeting.

"Thank you. I promise not to get in your way." He sips his coffee. "I'm sorry I didn't call you. I wanted to, but I didn't know what to say." He looks like he's been harboring a ton of guilt. I immediately understand what he's referring to and tears spring to my eyes.

"You have nothing to apologize for. I understand." I stand up and go to the sink. I can feel his eyes on me and blink away the tears. I turn back around to him. He gives me a small smile and stands. He comes over to me and puts his arms around me. I freeze. I can't believe he's hugging me. Instinctively, my arms go around him too. He places a kiss on the top of my head and holds me. He feels enormous next to my five foot three inches. He's so muscular, and I feel a jerk in my belly. Tears burn my eyes, and I can't hold them anymore. They spill down my cheeks.

"How are you?" He asks, still holding me to his chest.

I step out of his embrace and look up at him. I'm not one to wear my feelings on my sleeve, but with him, I can't stop it. For some reason, I can't hold it back from him.

"I have a huge hole in my heart. I miss them so much. People told me it would get better with time, but it hasn't. The crying lessens, and the pain dulls a little. You forget the day-to-day things, but it haunts me. I've tried therapy, but the nightmares are still there. I haven't slept more than three hours a night since the accident. I'll fall asleep and dream of the accident. I wake up in a panic all over again. It's as if it happens every single day. I've tried to move on with my life. I even changed my career." The tears fall as I speak, and he just listens. He doesn't try to offer comforting words, nor does he try to make it better for me. He just listens. Finally, after a few moments, he speaks.

"You'll never get over it. Your children, husband, and parents were ripped from you in such a horrible manner. It isn't fair, and no one deserves that kind of pain or to live through that kind of thing. I don't know what I would've done if I was in your shoes." He pauses for a moment like he's contemplating something. "Do you feel guilty you're still alive?" He asks.

"Yes. Every day I wonder if there's something I could've done differently but I come up empty. There's no way I could've stopped the drunk driver from hitting us. I just don't understand why I survived the crash." I turn out of his embrace and go to the window. I look out at the beach. I wrap my arms around myself for warmth. I suddenly feel so cold. I can feel Rey come up behind me.

"I'm sure you did everything you could. You can't change fate." He says soothingly. "Anything you need, I'm here for you. If you need to talk, I'll listen. If you need companionship, I'm here." He turns around and heads out of the kitchen. I turn and watch him pick up his suitcase and walk down the hall.

Chapter 3

A Glimpse into the Past

Kat

I was fourteen years old when I first saw him. He was my first crush. Reinaldo was a god to me. I was afraid to talk or look at him. He's five years older than I am, so I was a little girl to him for most of the time I crushed on him. We share an aunt and uncle, but there's no relation to each other. Uncle Manny is my uncle, and his wife is Reinaldo's aunt. Reinaldo's mother and my aunt are sisters. My parents and I used to go to my uncle's house for parties, Reinaldo and his parents were always there. Whenever we went to my uncle's house, I was excited and nervous. This went on for four years and he still hadn't noticed I was there. I saw him with various girls, and it tore me apart every time. Being he was so much older; we were at different stages in our lives.

When I was eighteen, we were invited to my cousin's graduation party at Uncle Manny's house. So, of course, we went. It was a hot June day. I wore jean shorts and a light blue t-shirt, tennis shoes without socks, and sunglasses. My hair was so long, and I let it hang down my back. The drive to the party felt like an eternity. We finally arrived, I stepped out of the car and started walking toward the house. Everyone was hanging out by the pool. I greeted everyone with hugs and kisses. I noticed Reinaldo wasn't there yet.

I got something to drink and sat on a chair near the pool watching the babies jumping in the water. I was one of the oldest of all my cousins, so I was usually by myself. A few minutes passed and my aunt, Lina, came and sat next to me. She was short with a pixie cut. She had brown eyes and pale skin. She has a big heart and is one of the nicest people you'll ever meet. I love this woman so much.

"Congratulations on graduating!" She said, smiling.

"Thank you. I'm so glad high school is over."

"You didn't like high school?" She seemed surprised by my comment.

"I hated it," I tell her.

"I'm surprised. Most kids are so upset to be getting out of high school."

"I know but I always felt high school was a waste of four years. I'm glad it's over and now I can study something that will lead me toward my career goals." I was always very mature, and I just didn't have anything in common with my peers. They liked to party, and I just wasn't into it. I worked, volunteered at the local hospital, and studied.

"I understand. You've always been a focused girl. I can't wait to see what's in store for you." She taps my hand and stands. "I just wanted to congratulate you. Now I have to go tend to the food."

"Thank you. I appreciate it. Do you need some help?" I ask.

"No, honey. You just relax and have a good time." She smiles and walks away.

I look back at the pool and watch as the kids splash around. I get up to refill my drink when Reinaldo walks through the door. He looks at me and I freeze.

"Hi, Kat." He says, smiling. He leans down and gives me a quick hug. The hug was long enough to feel the muscles in his back.

"Hi, Rey," I respond, smiling back. "How are you?"

"I'm doing okay. You?"

"I'm okay. It's nice to see you." I say quickly. I can hear my heart pounding and swear he can hear it too.

"Yeah, you too," he responds as some of the other guests walk up to him.

I walk to the drink table and refill my cup. I go back to my chair and continue to watch the kids in the pool. I pretend his presence doesn't faze me but all I want to do is watch every move he makes. I want to memorize everything about him.

****

Two hours later, a pool volleyball game is about to start. Teams are being formed. Rey is the captain of one team and my cousin, John, is the other team captain. John picks me for his team, so I go change into my bathing suit.

I walk into the bathroom and strip. I put on my suit and look in the mirror. *Yuck!* I have an hourglass figure with wide hips, a tiny waist, a big butt, and big boobs. I refuse to wear a normal bikini. I put on boy shorts and a tankini top. They, at the very least, cover me up nicely. I'm very conservative and self-conscious. I don't like to show too much cleavage and I don't wear shorts or skirts that are too short. I fish out my sunblock and apply it. I tie my hair up into a ponytail and head out to the pool.

Rey, John, and a few other people are already in the pool. I walk up the stairs and step into the pool. I bend my knees and sink into the water. It's warm and feels good on such a hot day. I look at Rey and notice he's watching me. He isn't smiling, just staring. His eyes lock on mine. Time stands still for a moment. He looks away and the game starts.

An hour later, the game ends, and Rey's team takes the win. We all high-fived each other, but when it was my turn, to high-five Rey, he pulls me into a hug. Before I can hug him back, he releases me. He smiles at me and climbs out of the pool. I get out of the pool, dry off, and change back into my clothes. The cake is cut and soon it's time to leave.

Rey is nowhere to be found. I don't get the chance to say goodbye.

****

Three years later, my parents and I visit Uncle Manny and Aunt Lina. There's no reason. We haven't seen them in a while and want to catch up. Paul and Luisa Vaz, Rey's parents, come over and we have dinner together. Luisa mentions Rey joined the Army and was doing well. I'm happy to hear he's doing well.

"Kat, he heard you would be here today and said he would pass by to say hello when he gets off work," Luisa says, smiling at me.

"Great," I respond and smile back. Nerves shot through me so fast I get dizzy. That's weird. Why would he come over here to visit me? He doesn't have any interest in me whatsoever. It's nice of him though. It'll be awesome to see him.

I get up to help my aunt with the dishes. As I'm carrying a stack of dirty plates to the sink, Rey walks through the door. *Oh my!* He's wearing black shorts and a blue button-down shirt. He looks sexy as hell. The Army has suited him. He was always built and crazy good-looking, but now there are no words. He's more built now and muscles bulge in his arms and chest. I stare at him. I'm rendered speechless. When I finally get my wits about me, I turn toward the kitchen.

I set the plates on the counter. He watches me with a huge grin on his face. I turn to him and smile back. I don't get the chance to say anything when his strong arms come around my waist. He pulls me to him and lifts me off my feet. My arms cling to his neck and I hug him back. He quickly sets me down.

"Hi," he says.

"Hi." My heart's beating so fast. I would give anything to be with this man, just to call him my boyfriend. I've wanted him for years and the way he just hugged me makes me want him so bad. "You look great."

"Thanks. You, too. How've you been?" he asks.

"I'm doing well. I hear you joined the Army," I say.

"Yes, I did, and I love it."

"Happy to hear it."

He winks at me and walks into the dining room to greet everyone else. The rest of the night goes by too quickly. Not another word is exchanged between us. I try not to stare at him, but I'll admit my gaze constantly falls on him. My mind wanders all night and I know I'm blushing most of the time I'm sitting there.

He kisses my cheek when he leaves, and I don't see him again.

Chapter 4

Rey

What the hell am I going to do? I sit on the bed and stare at the closed door. I never expected to see Kat here, much less share an apartment with her. *Oh, man! I have to plant a big wet one on Uncle Manny!!* I smile and stand up. I start unpacking my bags. That girl has been the object of my dreams for years. Now, I have a potential chance with her. I think the timing may finally be right for us.

I hate the sadness in her eyes though. She's trying to move on, but it looks like she's stuck. I look at the door again. She's lost so much weight but she's still absolutely gorgeous. She wears her hair to her shoulders and it's still that beautiful dirty blond. She has the most mesmerizing blue/gray eyes even though some of the light in them is gone. She isn't very tall but the perfect height. She has an hourglass figure that'll bring a man to his knees. A nice round butt hides with an oversized sweatshirt and baggy jeans. *Damn, she's sexy!* How am I going to keep my feelings in check? Keeping my hands off her may prove to be the hardest thing I've ever done.

I finish unpacking and place the bags under the bed. I sit down and stare at the door again. I've carried a torch for Kat since the first time I laid eyes on her but never said anything. I honestly believed I never had a chance with her. She's so out of my league. She's very educated and extremely smart. I've never had much interest in school. I have a degree but only because I knew I needed one.

But right now, I can't think about that. She needs a friend to help her move on. I'm going to be that friend. I'm going to help her and, maybe just maybe, we can have our chance. That is, of course, if she agrees. I frown. The most important thing right now is to help her. I want and need to bring happiness into her life again. I need to see the spark in her eyes.

****

Kat

I walk onto the balcony and sit down. Tears immediately fall as I look out. All my feelings for Rey come rushing back to me. *How can that happen? Will it be cheating on my husband? Would he want me to move on? But why am I feeling this guilt?* My husband's been dead for five years. Of course, he would want me to move on. He would want me to be happy. This isn't cheating but feels so wrong.

I bring my knees up and wrap my arms around them. The tears continue to fall as I stare at the water lapping the shore. The sound it makes is soothing, but my head and my heart are so full of turmoil. I hate having these feelings for someone who's never shown any feelings toward me. We were friends immediately but nothing ever romantic. *Why would he want me now? I'm broken. I've lost a lot of weight. I have these ugly black smudges under my eyes that haven't gone away since I lost my family. Why would he want to deal with my baggage? I wouldn't blame him. It's a whole lot of ugliness.*

I wipe my face and bury it in my knees. A moment later, I hear him walk onto the balcony and sit in the chair next to me.

"Are you okay?" He asks. "I know you've been up all night."

I look up but don't look at him. "Yeah. I'm sorry if I kept you up." He doesn't respond to that.

"You hungry?" He asks instead.

"I could eat." I look up at him. He's looking at me with a very pensive expression on his face. "You're not going to ask me why I'm out here crying?"

"No. You'll talk to me when you are ready to. Until then, I'm going to be your friend and try to get you to smile. You never know, you might have some fun. Let's go to grab some breakfast. My treat."

"You don't need to drag me along. I'm not much company." I tell him, still watching his face.

He smiles and stands. "I want you to join me." He holds out his hand.

I take it and stand. Sparks fly between our joined hands. I feel a bolt of electricity shoot up my arm. I look at his face, but he's looking at our hands. *Did he feel the same thing I did?* I release his hand. We walk inside and close the doors.

"I'll go get my purse," I say and go to my bedroom. A minute later, I'm pulling the strap of my purse over my head. Rey is standing by the front door.

"Ready?"

"Yes." He opens the door and waits for me to go ahead of him.

****

Twenty minutes later, we're sitting at a table that overlooks the beach. The restaurant sits on the water and is wrapped in windows. All the tables have a window view. We're seated directly in front of the ocean. It's going to be such a beautiful day. There isn't a cloud in the sky, but it's so cold. The sweatshirt and jeans are comfortable. But, then again, I didn't bring much else to wear. I need to go shopping sometime soon.

"What can I get you to drink?" The waitress asks and looks at me.

"Coffee, please," I tell her. She writes it down and looks at Rey. She smiles wide at him. I notice her check him out and shake my head. I don't blame her, but it irritates me since I'm sitting right here. She doesn't have any clue if we're together. But then again, she took one look at me and wouldn't believe a guy like Rey would be with me.

"Same for me." He says, and the waitress walks away.

I look back out the window and watch the waves. I can feel Rey's eyes on me. I look at him.

"What are your plans while you're here?" I ask. He's so gorgeous when he smiles like that. Those smiles are going to be the death of me. Those smiles light up the room and would make any woman's insides melt. It's not fair.

"Besides my cousin's wedding, I want to do some shopping, sightseeing and relax. I've needed a vacation. I haven't gone on one in a while because I never had anything to push me. When I got the wedding invitation, I jumped on coming here."

"Sounds like fun," I say. The waitress returns with two mugs and a coffee, sugar, and milk carafe. She sets them down on the table and takes our breakfast orders. Rey picks up the carafe and pours the coffee. I pour some sugar and milk into mine. I stir and bring the coffee to my mouth. I sip and close my eyes, savoring the rich brew.

"Are you planning to do anything specific while you're here? "He asks as he takes a sip of his coffee.

"Writing is the main objective. I thought I would do some shopping too."

"Sounds good. I read all three of your books." He says nonchalantly.

I stare at him. I can't believe he's read my books. I don't know what to say to him.

"Why are you staring at me like that? Are you surprised I read your books?"

"I'm sorry. I didn't know you knew I was writing. Plus, I didn't think you read that genre of books." I continue to watch his face. His lip quirks up as he answers me. Oh, man. When he does that with his lip, my stomach starts doing backflips. It's insane how this man makes my body respond to him.

"I don't read romances. I like suspense and mysteries. A few years ago, I was on leave visiting my parents. Before I left again, I stopped at the bookstore to pick up some of the latest new reads. I saw your first book and bought it. I read it in two days. It was great. You're an amazing writer. As I said, I don't read romances, but I read yours," he says, looking into my eyes. "I enjoyed my first romance novel."

I can see the sincerity in his eyes. He genuinely likes my writing. I feel my stomach clench. My eyes fill with tears. I try to blink them away but a few of them escape and run down my cheeks. He reaches across the table and places his hand on mine.

"I didn't mean to make you cry." He whispers.

I wipe my face with my free hand and say, "I know. I've been so alone for the last five years. I write to get out of my head, and I honestly didn't think of anyone reading my books. Besides my publisher and editor, you're the first to tell me you like my writing. Plus, I never thought you would have an interest in reading my books."

I look down at his hand over mine. It's so warm, and the simple touch carries so much comfort.

"Why wouldn't I be interested? I don't understand." He rubs his thumb on mine very gently. It's a sweet gesture and it makes me shudder. The clenching in my belly is getting stronger by the minute.

"I just figured you would do what my family did. Got the book but never actually read it." I'm still staring at our hands. He has strong hands. Long, thick fingers. A working man's hands. Very sexy hands that I want touching me.

"Anything that has to do with you, I'm interested in," he responds. "Plus, I believe you'll have your happily ever after soon."

I bring my eyes to his and stare into them.

"Thank you for your support," I say as the waitress walks up with our food. She places our plates in front of us.

"Can I get you anything else?" she asks.

"I think we're okay for now," Rey says, and she walks away. He never takes his eyes off mine.

He still has his hand on mine. He rubs my hand lightly and pulls away. "Eat up. You need some nourishment."

We eat our meal and talk about where he plans to go sightseeing.

Chapter 5

Kat

A half-hour later, we walk out of the restaurant and head back toward the apartment.

"When do you plan on working?" Rey asks.

"Tomorrow. I plan on taking the weekends off," I tell him.

"Great. Want to take a walk along the beach now? I plan on doing some shopping today. Would you like to join me?" He looks at me, waiting for my answer.

"Rey, please don't feel like you have to ask me to go."

"I know I don't have to. I like your company and I want you to come along. I wouldn't have asked if it's not what I wanted." He smiles wide.

"Okay. I would love to walk on the beach, and I could use some new clothes," I say, shrugging.

We step off the sidewalk, onto the sand, and head toward the water. We don't get too close to the water. I stop and pull off my tennis shoes. He watches me and pulls off his sneakers and socks, too. He stuffs his socks into his sneakers and ties his shoelaces together. He flings one sneaker over his shoulder. A shoe hangs on either side of his shoulder. I follow his lead. I tie my shoelaces together and hang my shoes on either side of my bag. I look at him and he laughs.

"Ready?" He asks.

"I am." We start walking. "It's such a beautiful day. It feels good to be outside." I'm in desperate need of fresh air and vitamin D.

"I take it you haven't spent much time outdoors lately?"

I'm looking down, watching my feet in the sand. "This is the first time I've been out. I only went to the grocery store," I say, and he looks at me. He stops walking.

"Seriously?" The look on his face is pure confusion.

"Yes. I was severely depressed, and I didn't want to deal with anyone. I almost committed suicide." I show him my wrist and watch his face fall. I can see the worry in his eyes. "I'm better. I'm still a little depressed. I realized I needed a change of scenery and needed to leave my house. What I almost did was a huge wake-up call."

"I'm glad you didn't do it," he says. "No malls, post office? Nowhere else but the grocery store?"

"I haven't been to a mall in five years. I haven't bought any new clothes since then either."

"Why not?" I can see he doesn't understand. We resume our walk as I explain.

"Shopping trips to the mall were something my mom and I loved doing. We would make it a whole Saturday thing. Even if we didn't buy anything, we would go store to store or window shop. We would take the kids and have lunch. We would have such a great time. When I lost them, the mall was such a painful place." His face changes and understanding.

"I'm sorry. Will you be okay today?" He asks.

"I think so. I need to get some new clothes. Badly. I'll think of her and the kids quite a bit, but I need to push through it. I need to move on. I need to function as a human being. This trip is to get out of my writer's block and hopefully return to normal life. I need to get out of my shell. I need to do this."

"You can do it. You're strong." He stuffs his hands into his pockets.

"If I was so strong, it wouldn't have taken me five years to leave my house. I feel like I lost myself. I'm very strong-willed and independent. Unfortunately, I let it get the best of me when the accident happened." He places his hand on my arm and stops me from walking. I look into his eyes. I see sadness and sympathy. I don't want him to feel sorry for me. I don't need to save.

"You've endured the worst thing anyone could endure. It's hard enough to lose a loved one, but five at once. It would break anyone. Honestly, I would've ended up in the looney bin." He takes a deep breath and runs a hand through his hair. "I understand why you contemplated suicide. I don't know what gave you the courage to stop but it shows the magnitude of your strength. I don't know if I could've stopped myself."

"I don't want you to feel sorry for me. I'm just starting to be okay. I still hurt but I'm coping the best I can." I cross my arms across my chest and look up at him.

"I don't feel sorry for you. I hurt for you. You've been through so much. I want to take away your pain. It isn't fair you have to live through that and live with it. I want to bear all the ugliness for you." His eyes swell with tears. His words touch my heart, and I can feel the stinging in my eyes.

"Why?" I ask as the tears spill uncontrollably. No one has ever said such a beautiful thing to me. His words touch me so deeply. He looks down at his feet and then back up. A tear spills from his eye. I can see all the emotion in his eyes. He takes a deep breath.

"I'm afraid to tell you why." He responds, looking directly into my eyes. I swear he can see right into my soul. "I want to be here for you and I'm afraid if you know the truth, you'll push me away. I don't want you to push me away. I finally have a chance to be a part of your life. I don't want to screw it up." Another tear spills from his eye. He wipes his face with the back of his hand, angrily.

"Tell me why. I won't run. I won't push you away. I promise."

He takes a deep breath. "I'm in love with you. I always have been."

I stop breathing. *What?* Did I just hear him correctly? He's never shown any interest and now he's in love with me. It doesn't make sense. I have so many questions, yet I can't get any words out. I'm staring at him like he's grown three heads.

"Say something, please." He says, nervously. I can see his hands shaking.

"If you've always felt that way, why didn't you ever say anything?" I wipe as another tear escapes.

"The timing was never right. When I first realized my feelings for you, you were eighteen and I was twenty-three. The age difference would've broken us. I was done with college and ready for the next step in life. You were just getting started with college and your adult life. Then, a few years later, you were still in school and dating someone. I didn't want to get in your way. So, I kept my mouth shut. I've lived my life carrying the secret."

"So, all these years, you decided it would be better to just not say anything? How was it better?" I ask, as I turn toward the water and sit down on the sand. I bring my legs up and wrap my arms around them. "I'm sorry, Rey. I just don't understand why you never said anything."

He sits down next to me. "I never said anything because I never wanted you to regret your life with me. If we tried a relationship when you were eighteen, you would've never experienced college the way I wanted you to. You were with someone, and I wasn't going to get in the middle of that. I wanted you happy and that took priority over what I felt." He crosses his arms over his knees and rests his chin on them. He watches the waves lapping the shore and waits for me to respond.

"I appreciate you kept my well-being as a priority and I realize you thought you were doing what you thought was best, but you made major decisions for me. I can make my own decisions. Do you realize if you had told me, all those years ago, my life could be so different right now?" I look at him. He's looking at me, hanging on every word falling from my lips.

"No. I didn't think about that." He says and looks back toward the slapping waves. I can tell he's thinking about what I just asked.

"I understand why you did it. I'm not mad or upset. I wish you hadn't decided for me though. If you had asked, I would've said yes. I wouldn't have thought twice about it. But you didn't, and I was meant to go through what I did," I say. "I now know I can get through anything. I might not look it, but I don't break easily. The depression I went through was my way of handling the situation. I made myself get through it."

"You're tenacious. I admire how you've handled and continue to handle everything," he says, looking at me.

"I don't want admiration. I want and need a friend. I don't have anyone and I'm lonely." I scratch my forehead. "I can't believe I just said that."

"I'm always here for you. You don't have to be lonely anymore." He places his hand on mine. "Always tell me what you feel. Don't ever be embarrassed. You're the best person I know and nothing you say will change that."

"As far as your confession goes, I've always dreamed of hearing those words from you. You were always the one that got away. But I'm not ready for that yet. It could come quickly, or it might take a while before I can say those words back to you. I don't expect you to wait," I say, being as honest as I can be.

"Are you kidding? I've been waiting all these years and if there is even just a slim chance you'll love me back, then hell yes, I'll wait for you. Take as long as you need it. I promise I'll never pressure you. I just want to be with you." He smiles at me. He still hasn't moved his hand off mine. I pull my hand away.

I stand up and brush the sand off my ass. He does the same.

"Let's go shopping."

"I have one more question," he says.

"What's that?"

"When will I see you smile? I haven't seen you smile and it's scaring the shit out of me."

"I don't know," I respond, and we start walking. "I think I've forgotten how to smile."

Chapter 6

Kat

Three hours later, we're sitting at an outdoor café. We both have a bottle of water and a sandwich in front of us. The other two empty chairs are covered in shopping bags.

"Did you find everything you were looking for?" Rey asks.

"I did. I just have one more store to hit and I'm done." I say and take a sip of water.

"Which store is that?"

"The lingerie store," I answer, blushing. He smiles but tries to hide it by taking a bite out of his sandwich. I bite into mine as well. "How about you?"

"I have to go to the suit store. My good suit is back in the states, so I need to buy another one for the wedding. I don't think the one in the states would fit me anymore anyway," he says.

I nod my understanding. "Those two stores are right next to each other, so it works out. I'm sorry if I dragged you around today."

"You didn't. I'm having a lot of fun," he says and takes another bite of his sandwich.

"I'm glad. I'm having fun too. I'd forgotten what fun was." I look up at him and he gives me a small smile.

"You just gave me the most amazing gift," he says.

"What? I don't understand." I'm staring at him now.

"You're having fun and it makes me happy. Showing you how to have fun again is a gift you allowed me," he says and visibly swallows hard. "Will you be my date for my cousin's wedding?"

My head snaps up from looking down at my plate. "What? Are you sure?"

"Of course. Why wouldn't I be?" he asks.

"Don't you have to ask your cousin first?"

"If you agree to come with me, I'll call him right now. He told me to bring a date. I RSVP'd for just one but can easily change that. Please come with me."

"Okay," I whisper. I look down at my plate and start to panic a little. I have a lot to do to myself to get ready for a wedding.

He reaches into his pocket and pulls out his phone. He scrolls through his contacts and presses the send button. I continue eating while Rey speaks to his cousin. His cousin is okay with me accompanying Rey to the wedding. He finishes the call and smiles at me.

"Make that two more stores to go to," I say.

Rey laughs, and we finish our lunch.

****

We're headed back to the apartment after a few more hours. I'm carrying a garment bag with the dress and another two bags in my hand. Rey carries another garment bag and a bag in each hand, as well.

"Give me your bags," Rey says as he reaches for the bags in my hand.

"No, you're carrying enough already. I can carry it. Thanks," I respond.

"At least let me have your garment bag."

"I'm okay. We're almost home anyway," I tell him without breaking my stride.

"You're stubborn," he says and smiles wide.

"Yes, I am," I agree.

"Did you find everything you wanted?" he asks.

"Yes, I did. It was a lucky shopping day. I don't think shopping has ever been this easy for me," I say. "How about you?"

"I did. Now I don't need to worry and can relax."

"Same here. One less thing on my mind. I've been worrying about going shopping. Your invitation gave me the push I needed. Thank you for spending the day with me and helping me make that leap. If only I could get past this writer's block."

"I'm sure it'll go away soon. Do you want to shoot me some ideas? Maybe it might get the juices flowing." He looks at me and I sneak a look at him.

"Thank you. That actually might work. I'll share some of my ideas while I cook dinner. I'm thinking chicken soup," I say.

"That sounds amazing. The perfect dinner after a busy day like today plus the temperature is dropping."

We continue to walk and talk. Ten minutes later, we're about two blocks from the apartment when he tells me to continue to the apartment. He's going to stop for dessert. I continue walking and, within five minutes, I'm entering the apartment. I walk to my bedroom and open the closet. I hang the garment bag and place the bags on the floor of the closet. I walk to the kitchen, wash my hands, and start prepping dinner.

****

Rey

Ten minutes later, I walk into the apartment. The smell coming from the kitchen is mouthwatering. I quickly drop my bags in my bedroom and stop in the kitchen doorway. Kat's at the stove stirring the contents in a pot. I watch her for a minute. She's so sexy, and she looks so comfortable in the kitchen. That figure of hers blows me away. She has beautiful dirty blond hair, but she keeps it pulled up in a ponytail all the time now. I still can't believe the day we had together. The sadness is still in her eyes, but it seems to have diminished a little.

Talking and shopping with her was a lot of fun. She's funny even when she doesn't smile or laugh. I can't imagine how much fun she would be if she never endured the ugliness of the accident. She's an amazing woman. I wish I could take away the pain. She doesn't deserve it.

She moves away from the stove to grab a spoon. She tastes the contents in the pot. She nods and washes the spoon.

"Hi," I say, and she turns around. She yelps in surprise.

"Hi," she says, gripping her chest. I step into the kitchen and place a white box and a bottle of wine on the kitchen table. "You didn't need to stop for wine. I have some."

"I wasn't sure, so I bought a bottle anyway." I go to the cupboard and grab two wine glasses. As I open the bottle, I can feel her watching me, but she doesn't say anything. I pour the wine into the glasses and hand her a glass.

"Thank you," she says, taking it. She takes a sip. "Mmm. It's really good."

"You're welcome." I take a sip. "You're right. It is good."

"The soup will be ready in about half an hour."

"Perfect," I say. "The wedding is next Saturday, and I'm making a reservation at a hotel for two nights.

I'm planning on leaving Friday and returning on Sunday. It's about a three-hour drive and I don't want to rush Saturday morning. I don't want to worry about driving after the wedding. Is it okay if I make you a hotel reservation as well?" I ask nervously. I don't want to freak her out or make her uncomfortable. She watches me intently.

"Yes, please. I'll give you my credit card so you can do that," she responds.

"No way. I asked you to come with me. I'll take up the cost," I say. I'm leaning against the door jam and she's leaning against the counter. She shakes her head.

"I appreciate it, but I can't let you do that. I want to go and there's no reason for you to pay for my hotel room. I also want to pay half of the car rental and gas," she says.

I step closer to her and lean against the counter next to her.

"I don't want to seem old-fashioned, but you're not paying for half of the car rental or gas. I was already getting this before you were coming with me. I can't take your money. I want to pay for your room. You're doing me the honor of being my date. It's the least I can do." I watch her face and I see the defeat in her eyes.

"You know you don't have to do it even though I do appreciate it. I'm your date because I want to be not because I expect you to pay for everything. Can you let me pay for the meals and half of the gift please?" she pleads.

"Okay. Compromise. You pay for the meals, and I'll take care of the gift." I smile at her, and she shakes her head at me.

"You're impossible," she says and turns toward the stove. She stirs the soup slowly.

"It smells incredible," I say, stepping behind her. I can smell her shampoo from where I stand and it's driving me crazy. It smells of lavender. I want to take the elastic out of her hair and watch it spill down her back. I want to run my hands through it. But, of course, I don't. She reaches for the clean spoon and dips it into the pot.

"Want to try it?" she asks.

"Absolutely." She turns with a spoon in her hand. She places her other hand under the spoon so nothing will spill and blows gently to cool it. She brings the spoon up toward my lips. I open my mouth and she places the spoon on my tongue. I close my lips around the spoon, and she pulls it out slowly. Her cheeks flush as she watches my mouth.

"Wow! That's good," I say, licking my lips.

She watches me lick my lips and turns quickly toward the sink. I see the blush appear on her cheeks. She washes the spoon, and I can see her taking a few deep breaths. I can't help the smile that makes its way to my lips.

"I'm glad you like it," she says but doesn't at me.

"Do you want to eat on the balcony?" I ask. She nods her answer. "I'll set the table."

Chapter 7

Kat

Twenty minutes later, we're eating our soup. We sit quietly for a while and it's comfortable. I want to kiss Rey. I want to thank him for making me feel something again. Because of him, I had fun today. I'm anticipating going to the wedding next weekend and I'm a bit nervous too. I haven't felt anticipation since the accident. I haven't felt any kind of emotion since the accident. I didn't anticipate any of the book releases I've had. I just went through the motions, like a robot. I finally have some hope for the future. I think I may just get through this.

"Are you okay?" He asks, interrupting my thoughts. I look up from my soup, startled by the sound of his voice. I was so caught up in my thoughts.

"Yes."

"You just seem so far away." He says, seemingly searching my face.

"Sorry. I was just thinking about today." I explain.

"I had a great day." He smiles at me. That smile melts my insides every time. It lights up his whole face and I can see he truly enjoyed himself.

"I did too. Thank you." I take a sip of my wine and look at him. I give him a small smile. It feels so strange on my face. "I had fun and it felt good." Rey stares at me. His smile falters.

"Is that a smile I see?" he asks.

I nod. "It is. You put it there."

"No need to thank me. I should be thanking you. I haven't had that much fun in a long time. Seeing you smile again makes me the happiest man alive right now." I can see he's being serious. His eyes show me how sincere he is.

"That's why I'm thanking you. Smiling was something I forgot to do. I haven't felt the need for it in five years. I just went day to day. I forgot what having fun is like. I forgot what hope is. I didn't care what happened to me. I didn't want to think of the future," I say, taking a deep breath. "I want to find happiness again but a part of me feels so guilty I can."

"Why do you feel guilty?" he asks.

"I lost my whole family. I shouldn't want happiness. I feel like I'm betraying them." I feel the tears sting my eyes. I try to blink them away, but one escapes and rolls down my cheek.

He places his hand on mine. His hand is so warm and feels so good on my skin.

"You have nothing to feel guilty about. Your family would want you happy regardless of the circumstances. The accident wasn't your fault. You didn't die. Therefore, God wanted to give you another chance in life. I don't know why this was your fate, but it was. It totally sucks and if I could take away the pain, I would."

Now the tears fall uncontrollably. I pull my hand away and wipe my face with my napkin.

"I know you're right. I just can't push the guilt away." I try to gain some resolve.

"What will help you get rid of the guilt?" he asks. I can see he'll do anything to help me. He has no idea how much I appreciate having him here with me. He's not judgmental or tells me to move on. He's patient and understanding. He'll never know how much he's done for me in such a short time.

"I don't know," I respond, and he takes a deep breath.

"I want to say something, but I don't know how to say it. I'm just going to say it." He takes another deep breath as if gathering the courage. "I think we have our second chance. I want you, every part of you. I want you in my life again. I missed my chance years ago to be with you and now I feel like I'm getting another one. I'm not going to throw it away. Someone or something brought us together. I won't push you or force anything on you. I promise you, but I'm not going to let this opportunity go without a fight."

"I agree we have a second chance, but I need some more time. I wish I could give you a timeline. I won't lie to you…I want you to. I want us to have a life together," I say. *Did I just tell him that? What the hell is wrong with me?* He shakes his head.

"We have all the time in the world. There's no pressure." He takes a sip of his wine. "You tell me when you're ready for the next step. You're in control."

I give him a weak smile again. "Thank you."

He nods. "Want to watch some TV?"

"Sure." I start to pick up the dishes. He places a hand over mine and pushes the dishes back onto the table.

"You cooked. I'll clean." He picks up the dishes and heads into the kitchen.

I watch him go. My stomach is in knots. I want him so bad, but my brain won't let me let go of the guilty thoughts. I still can't believe I admitted my feelings for him. I find it so easy to talk to him. He makes me comfortable, and words spill out of my mouth around him. I need some sign to let me know it's okay to move on.

****

I roll over in bed. The clock reads 2:15 AM. *The usual time.* I stare at the ceiling. My mind is racing. I can't collect my thoughts. Having Rey sleeping in the room next door is messing with my insides. It's been so long that I forgot those parts existed. All I want to do is crawl into bed next to him and wrap my arms around him. *I can't think about this.* To calm my thoughts, I do what I usually do in the middle of the night.

I reach over, turn on the bedside lamp, and sit up. I pick up the book sitting on the bedside table and start to read.

A few minutes later, I hear a knock at my door.

"Come in," I say. The door opens slowly, and Rey leans against the door jam. He's wearing a pair of shorts and a t-shirt. I stare at him. My mouth is suddenly dry. I try to pull my eyes away, but I can't.

"Are you okay?" he asks.

"Yes." I clear my throat. "What are you doing up?" He crosses his arms in front of his chest.

"I'm a light sleeper and heard movement. I woke up and saw your light on, so I decided to check on you," he explains.

"I only sleep a few hours a night. This is the usual time I wake up every night. I spend many nights frustrating myself trying to sleep. So, I decided to just get up and read when I woke up. I've had this problem since the accident," I tell him and shrug like it's no big deal.

"Wow. How many hours of sleep do you get a night?"

"No more than three." He shakes his head.

"So, you read until when?" He has a shocked expression on his face.

"I read until five, get up, and get dressed. I go for a run. After the run, I work."

"When I was deployed in Iraq, I went two weeks sleeping no more than three hours and once it caught up to me, I was worthless. I don't know how you've done it for five years. Have you tried taking something to help you sleep?" He asks.

"No. I'm so afraid to get hooked on pills."

"Do you mind if I join you on your morning runs? I run at that time too."

"Sure, I would love it," I say, and he smiles.

"Well, enjoy your book. I'm going to go back to bed." He straightens and grabs the door handle.

"Good night," I say, watching him retreat. He has a great ass.

"Good night," he says and closes the door.

Chapter 8

Kat

This last week has flown by. Today has gone by extremely fast, as well. The early morning run was great. We ran two miles and stopped for coffee. We came back to the apartment and Rey made breakfast while I showered. We ate, I cleaned up, and I started working. I was able to get a complete outline. It was a very productive day. I got the idea for my new book while running and when I sat down to outline, the ideas just flowed. Hopefully, the writing will go as smoothly as the outline went.

It's ten to five and I'm sitting at the table, rereading, and editing my outline when Rey walks in. I turn toward the door, and he offers me a big smile. I give him a small smile back and watch as he makes his way to the table.

"Hi," he says.

"Hi. How was your day?" I ask.

"Great. How was yours?"

"I got the outline done," I tell him. "An idea came to me during our run this morning. Once I started the outline, ideas started flowing."

"That's great!" He sits next to me. "So, is the writer's block over?"

"I won't know for sure until I start writing but I hope so. My publisher's emails haven't been very friendly."

"Let me take you to dinner to celebrate."

"That sounds great," I say and close my laptop. I organize the sheets of paper in front of me. "Let me go change and we can go."

"I'm thinking we should go to the restaurant in the casino," he says.

"I haven't been to the casino."

"Neither have I, but I've heard great things about the restaurant. We can have dinner, walk around, and do some gambling." He looks so happy.

"I'm not a gambler but I'll play a slot or two for fun," I say.

"Great. Go get ready. I'll take the bathroom after you." I nod and get moving.

In the bathroom, I turn on the water in the shower and look at my reflection in the mirror. Ugh. I look terrible. *How the hell am I supposed to get dressed up for a nice dinner when I have these ugly bags under my eyes and my hair hasn't been styled in years?* I guess I'm just going to have to do my best. It's been a while and I don't know if I remember how to fix myself up. Rey knows what I look like and obviously, he doesn't care that I look awful. I shrug, undress, and get into the shower.

Ten minutes later, I'm in my room, staring at my closet. I pull the black maxi dress out and lay it on the bed. I pull out black flats and grab the blow dryer I took from the bathroom on my way out. I head toward the other bathroom and start styling. A few minutes later, I'm staring at the mirror trying to figure out how to apply my makeup. I don't know what I'm doing anymore. I had to buy all new makeup and applying it was going to be a challenge. I do the best I can and head back to my room. I slip on the dress. I take a final look in the mirror. I pick up the little clutch purse and open my bedroom door. *Here goes nothing.*

****

A few minutes earlier…

Rey

I watch as Kat walks into her bedroom, and I head into the kitchen. I grab a beer. I open it, take a long pull, and walk onto the balcony. I lean against the railing on my forearms and look out at the ocean. Kat looked so happy when I walked in. Her face completely lit up when she told me she had the outline done. The relief she was feeling was palpable. I wish I could get rid of the blackness under her eyes though. I sure as hell don't like her insomnia. I hear the bathroom door open and turn. I see her step out in a long fluffy white robe and her hair is wrapped in a towel. She walks quickly into her bedroom and closes the door. I can't help but smile as I watch her. My conservative girl. I've barely seen any part of her skin exposed.

I quickly finish my beer, throw the bottle into the trash, and head for the shower. While I wash up, I think of Kat. I wonder how long it'll take to break her out of her shell. For fifteen years, I have dreamt of her. I've dreamed of kissing her and having passionate nights with her. I've had dreams of having a family with her. I have my chance now, but would she want the same thing? She's so broken but in the last couple of days, she seems to want to make a change. She gave me a small smile, finally. She was honest with me and admits she wants me. I can understand why but I fear the loss of my restraint. Leaning in to kiss her or holding her hand would only scare her further. I can't bear the thought of not having a future with her when it's right in front of my face. For the first time in a very long time, I'm hopeful for the future. *God, please lead me in the right direction with her. Please help her push away her fears and take on a chance.* A chance my shower and dry myself off. I tie the towel around my waist, brush my teeth, and open the bathroom door. I peek around and make sure Kat's door is still closed. I swiftly dash to my bedroom and close the door. I pull a pair of boxer briefs out of the dresser and put them on. At my closet, I decide on a pair of black slacks and a maroon button-down shirt. Next, I put on my socks and dress shoes. I look in the mirror. My hair is so short I don't need to do anything to it. I take a deep breath and walk out of my bedroom. I sit down at the kitchen table and flip through a magazine when I hear Kat's door open. I stand and step out of the kitchen. She's walking toward me and my heart stops beating. I'm speechless.

***

Kat

I step out of my bedroom and walk toward the kitchen when Rey steps out. *Oh my! He looks gorgeous! How the hell am I going to keep my eyes off him?* He stops short when he sees me. I keep walking until I'm standing in front of him. His eyes rake my body and back up to meet mine. Heat rushes through me. My heart feels like it's going to beat right out of my chest.

"You look gorgeous," he says. I can feel my face flush.

"Thank you. You look great too." My cheeks feel so hot. It must be the color of his shirt.

"You're even sexier when you blush." He smiles at me. I don't know what to say to that. I look down at my shoes to try to gain some composure. This man stirs feelings inside me I haven't felt in many years, nor do I know what to do with them. It's nice to know my lady parts still work.

When I look back up at him, he's just watching me.

"I'm sorry if I pushed too hard. You blow my mind." He isn't smiling but watching my reaction.

"You didn't and thank you. I had a hard time getting ready. I haven't fixed my hair or my makeup in five years, so I'm very much out of practice. I appreciate you being so kind," I say.

"Sweetheart, I'm not being kind. I'm telling the truth. You're the most beautiful woman I've ever laid eyes on. From the first moment I saw you, I couldn't take my eyes off you." I blush again and gave him a weak smile. "Are you ready to go?" he asks.

"Yes." We walk to the front door and head out.

Chapter 9

Kat

Dinner was amazing. We had a light conversation about our childhoods, schooling, and what Rey does in the military. The restaurant is beautiful, and the food was delicious. Rey has been a complete gentleman. He pulls out the chair for me, opens the doors, and treats me like I'm the only woman in the world. Other women are constantly checking him out, but he's oblivious to them. He listens to every word I say, and I can tell he's truly interested in what I have to say. My stomach has had butterflies since the minute I saw him standing in the apartment. Why am I so scared to show this man how I feel about him? Everyone I love is dead and I'm not for a reason. Why am I living my life like I'm dead? My family wouldn't want that for me. They would want me to be happy. Rey's the key to my happiness, yet I'm so scared I'll lose him too. I've wanted him from a very young age, and it didn't happen. We went our separate ways and I found love with a great man. We married, had children, and a drunk driver took them all away. Now, the man I first crushed on and wanted is back in my life. I can't and won't let him go this time.

The waitress comes over to our table and cleans up the empty dishes. She smiles at Rey.

"Care for dessert?" she asks him. He doesn't look up at her.

"Do you want dessert?" he asks me with a wide smile.

"I do, but I can't have the whole thing by myself. We can share something if you want."

"Do you like tiramisu?"

"My favorite," I say.

"We'll have one tiramisu with two forks and two cappuccinos," he tells the waitress.

"No problem. It'll be out in a few minutes." She walks away.

There's a live band playing in the restaurant. The casino is mostly Americanized. The staff at the restaurants all speak English and the menus are a mix of the cuisine. The band only seems to play American music and each song being played is romantic. The band prefers country love songs which I don't mind. There's a small dance floor in front of the band. Every time I look over, couples are dancing to a new song.

Rey stands and walks over to me. He puts his hand out. "May I have this dance?" he asks.

I place my hand in his and stand. "Yes."

He places his hand on the small of my back and leads me to the dance floor. As we walk, I recognize the song. It's "Wanted" by Hunter Hayes. Once on the dance floor, I place my hand on his shoulder and the other hand is enveloped in his. His arm comes around my waist and brings our hands to rest on his chest near his heart. I can feel the beat of his heart against my hand. He leans his head down so he can whisper in my ear.

"This song is for you. Every time I hear it, I think of you." He leans his head to mine as we sway to the music. I close my eyes and listen to the lyrics of the song. It's a beautiful song and the dance is over much too quickly. I love being held by him. I feel so safe and comfortable. It's as if I'm made to be in his arms.

The song ends, and we break apart. We walk back to our table. Again, he pulls out my chair and I sit. As soon as he sits, the waitress appears with our dessert and coffee. She sets them down and walks away.

I pick up my coffee mug and take a sip.

"That's a really good cappuccino," I tell him. Rey picks up his mug and takes a sip.

"You're right. It is." He smiles at me.

We dig into the tiramisu. I take a bite and close my eyes. A small moan escapes my lips as I savor the rich flavors invading my tongue.

"Oh wow! That's incredible!" I say, thoroughly enjoying the cake. When I open my eyes, Rey's staring at me. "What? Do I have some on my chin?" I quickly grab my napkin and wipe my chin.

"No. Um…" He clears his throat. "I'm glad you're enjoying the cake." He sets his fork down.

"You're not having anymore?" He seems fidgety now.

"Yes, I am." He takes a deep breath. "I…I just need a minute." He picks up his coffee and takes a sip.

"Are you okay?" I'm starting to worry. I've never seen him so uneasy. He looks like he's going to jump up and bolt at any minute.

"Yes. I'm sorry. I'm okay." He takes another deep breath.

"Okay, but just know you can tell me anything. If I did something you didn't like, please tell me." I'm watching him very intently now. He seems to have calmed down some.

"You didn't do anything I didn't like. You turned me on so much I had to remind myself to keep my composure. Watching you take that bite of the cake made me crazy," he tells me. His eyes are darker, and I can see the want. I stare back at him in surprise. That's the last thing I expected him to say. My cheeks feel hot, and I know my face is a dark shade of red.

"I'm sorry. I didn't deliberately mean to do that." I look down at my hands on my lap.

"Kat, look at me." I do as he asks. "You do it to me. Period. Everything you do drives me insane. I want you so bad. I want to touch you, but I don't want to push you or rush you in any way. So, I have to remind myself to keep my composure. The dance we just shared was amazing. Having you in my arms felt too good, so right. The next thing I know you're taking a bite of cake and closing your eyes in absolute pleasure and the moan that escaped your lips nearly brought me to my knees. Any man would lose his cool watching you. You have no idea how beautiful you are. You're unbelievably sexy and you don't even realize it. It makes you even sexier. I'm sorry…I probably shouldn't have said all that but now you know. I can't bear for you to think you did something wrong or think I'm upset with you." He gives me a small smile. My mind is whirling with what he just told me. *He thinks I'm sexy. Has the man looked at me? I'm way too thin, my hair needs color and styling, I need a refresher on how to apply makeup, and I need to sleep. Not to mention all the baggage I'm carrying around.*

"You're right. The dance we just shared was amazing. Thank you for dedicating the song to me. I also need to tell you that being in your arms made me feel so safe. For those few minutes, I didn't think about anything but you. Since the moment I saw you standing in the apartment, my insides have not stopped stirring." I take a deep breath. Tears threaten in my eyes. I blink them away and continue. "You stir feelings inside me I forgot existed. I want to be with you more than you know. I've always wanted to be with you, but it's never been the right time for us. Now we have our chance, but I'm all messed up. I need to figure out a way to let this guilt go so I can move on. It isn't fair to either of us. I promise you I'll do what I can. Until then, please be patient with me." I say as a tear falls down my cheek. I quickly wipe it away. My napkin is on the table, and I place my hand on it in case I need it.

Rey places his hand over mine lightly. His hand is so strong and warm. Hard-working hands that are callused, yet soft. "I'm not going anywhere. I know we only have a short time here, but I'm not letting you go. Not this time. Take all the time you need. There's no rush. You tell me when you're ready."

I give him a small smile. "Let's finish dessert and go explore the casino."

He laughs. "Good idea."

Chapter 10

Kat

Last night was a night I'll never forget. Although I felt awkward, Rey was a perfect gentleman and made the night magical. After he paid for dinner, we walked around exploring the casino. Rey and I played a few slots, and I won two hundred euros. Rey lost about forty. I teased him about it most of the night. He took the teasing in stride and made me laugh a few times. Hearing myself laugh again was surreal and foreign, but it felt good. We continued to explore, did some window shopping, and decided it was time to call it a night. We walked through the front door at midnight. I fell into bed and slept until three, yet again.

At five, I got out of bed for my usual morning run and Rey was already waiting for me. We ran and he made breakfast. I sit down and open my laptop. I finish proofreading my outline by the time breakfast is ready. After breakfast, I start writing and Rey lies on the couch reading a book.

At noon, Rey gets up off the couch and goes into the kitchen. I'm on a roll writing and wasn't ready to stop. A few minutes later, he sits a plate down next to my computer. On the plate are a sandwich and sliced-up strawberries. Next to the plate, he places a can of diet cola. He places a hand on my shoulder and squeezes. He heads out onto the balcony to eat his lunch. He continues reading his book while he eats.

"Thank you," I yell out. He smiles at me.

"You're welcome," he says. I love that he understands I don't want to stop writing. He understands how important it is and gives me the space I need.

At three, I decided I'm done for the day and come to a good stopping point. If I keep this pace, I'll be done writing the book within three weeks. I close my laptop and stand. I stretch. I look out at the balcony and Rey's still sitting in the same chair with his feet up on the railings. He's watching the ocean now. He looks deep in thought, and I contemplate whether or not I should disturb him. I decide to go out there to make sure he's all right. I walk out there and sit in the chair next to him. He looks over at me.

"Are you okay?" I ask.

"Yes, of course. Do I not look okay?"

"You look deep in thought," I say, searching his eyes. I don't see stress or nervousness in them.

"I was just thinking about what places to visit next," he says.

"Oh. Any ideas?"

"No. Unfortunately, it's been so long since I've been here. I have no idea where to go. I'll go to the travel agency down the street tomorrow."

"I'd love to take a look around the cathedral we pass on our run every morning," I tell him.

"I've wanted to go look at it, too."

"Let's go." I stand up. He looks up at me and contemplates it for a minute.

"Let's go," he repeats and stands.

****

Twenty minutes later, we're walking into the cathedral. It's magnificent. It's built out of rock and has about fifty wooden pews facing the altar. The altar has statues depicting the nailing of the cross. It's gruesome yet very beautiful. All the statues around the church and the accents are in gold. We walk up to the altar, and I kneel on the step leading up. Rey stands next to me looking around. I close my eyes, bow my head, and begin to pray. I feel Rey kneel next to me. We kneel there praying for a few minutes. I feel him get up and start to walk around the church. I continue to pray.

God, please help me to move on. I've been stuck in this guilty place for so long. I don't know why you didn't take me when you took my family but here I am. I know my family would want me to go on with my life but I'm finding it very difficult. I have a lot of faith in you and how I'm able to be here today. You know that. I need your help now though. Rey's back in my life. I don't know how we were brought together but I'm grateful. We finally have our chance, but I can't move forward. I feel like I'm cheating on my husband and turning my back on my kids. I know they passed, and I know it isn't true, but I can't move past it. I need to know it's okay to move on. I need to know this guilt I'm feeling is unwarranted.

I bring my face up and look toward the heavens. I can't stop the tears from falling down my face. I stare at the statues on the altar but can't focus on them. My vision is blurry, and I close my eyes again. Suddenly, I feel a light breeze come across my face. I take a deep breath and I feel it again. I open my eyes and I don't have any more tears. I stand up quickly and turn to see where Rey is. He's in the back admiring the organ. I smile, and for the first time since my family died, I don't feel any guilt. My heart starts to beat rapidly. I turn around and look up toward the ceiling. *Thank you.*

I look to my right and see the candle table. I walk over and light a stick. I light five candles. *My babies-I hope you're happy. I love and miss you both so much. Sometimes it's hard to breathe. Please give mommy the strength to move forward. I'm stuck and need a good push. Sweetheart, I hope you're at peace. Please give our babies kisses for me. I miss you and love you but it's time for me to gain a grasp on my life. I hope you understand and you're happy for me. Mom and Dad, I hope you both are at peace too. I love and miss you very much. I need your guidance and protection. For five years, I've been closed off to everything and everyone around me. I can't live like that anymore. The five of you are my guardian angels and I know you're smiling down on me now. Thank you for guiding me in the right direction.*

I turn and walk to the back of the church. Rey's now sitting in a pew, waiting for me. I walk up to him and reach for his hand.

"Are you ready?" I ask him. He looks down at my hand and places his hand in mine.

"Yes," he says and stands. We walk to the doors, and I stop. I link my fingers through his. He watches our hands and smiles wide. I look toward the altar one more time. I give Rey a real smile as I look up at him. He brings his other hand up to my face and runs his thumb along my bottom lip.

We walk out of the church with our hands linked together.

Chapter 11

Kat

It's a beautiful day. It's sunny and breezy and there isn't a cloud in the sky. Suddenly, I'm appreciating my surroundings. I'm aware of the weather and how lucky I am to be able to see it and experience everything around me. I only went through the motions for the last five years. I only paid attention to the weather when I was hot or cold, only to change my clothing. Right now, I'm enjoying the beauty I'm looking at. I'm enjoying the feel of the sun on my face. We're walking on the beach, hand in hand. It feels so right and I'm not feeling any guilt about it. I'm thinking clearly, and I now know why I had the thought to come to Portugal. I was destined to be on this path and now it's my time to move on. I needed to experience the last five years and now I can be free of it.

Rey lifts our linked hands to his mouth and kisses my hand. The warmth that spreads through my body feels good. I love how Rey makes me feel. My body awakens, and my mind is free. I don't have to hide anything from him.

"Not that I'm complaining and trust me, I'm not, but what brought this on?" he asks. I stop walking and turn to him.

"Today was the first time I visited a church since the accident. I always had my faith, but I didn't go to church. I wanted to go to church but was afraid to. I don't know why I was afraid, but I was. When you said you wanted to go, you gave me the push I needed. I was too chicken to go alone." I stop and take a deep breath. Rey's hanging on my every word. "When we walked into the church, I immediately felt a certain peace I haven't felt in a very long time, maybe never."

Rey nods. "I felt the same peace."

"When I knelt at the altar, I decided to take a different prayer approach. Until now, I would say the prayers we were taught as kids, but never took the time to speak to God. Today, I decided to pour my heart out. I put it all out there and when I was done, I asked God to give me some sign I should move on without the guilt. I looked up when I was done and felt a light breeze on my face. It was a breeze I'd never felt before. It happened again a second time and I knew it was the sign I had asked for. I thanked Him, walked over to the candles, and lit five. I spoke to my children, husband, and parents and asked them to be my guardian angels." Tears swell in my eyes at the memory. I try to blink them away but fail. A tear streams down my face. "I know it might sound crazy, but I feel at peace now."

Rey wipes the tear away with his free hand and flattens his palm on my face. His hand is so warm, and I lean my face into it. I close my eyes and savor his touch. When I open my eyes, I find him staring at me.

He leans down and places his lips on mine. His lips are so soft and warm yet firm. He applies the slightest bit of pressure and pulls away. I open my eyes slowly, a little stunned.

"I'm sorry. I couldn't help myself," he says. "I hope it was okay."

"It's more than okay. I liked it," I tell him, and he smiles.

"I'm so glad you were able to find the answers you needed visiting that church. You didn't have to ask your family to be your guardian angels. They already are and will continue to be. I need you to understand I'll never get upset if you want to talk about them. I will get upset if you don't share those thoughts and feelings. I want to be a part of everything that's you. Don't hold anything back and I won't hold anything from you. Your husband and children were your life. I want you to share stories about them."

"You make me happy," I respond.

"You make me happy, too. I cannot wait to see what our future has in store for us."

"Me too."

He pulls my hand, and we continue to walk. He drops my hand and places his arm around my shoulders. He brings me closer and places a kiss on my temple. My arm links around his waist. We walk that way all the way home.

Chapter 12

Kat

The next morning, after our usual run, Rey makes breakfast. I start working and hear the TV clicking on in the kitchen. I hear the news anchor start a report about the cold weather that will be heading our way. I stop writing to listen. The meteorologist describes the frigid weather that will happen tonight. He speaks about extremely cold temperatures for the next few nights. He warns about the dangers of the cold without heat. Rey comes to the kitchen doorway and announces breakfast is ready. I save my work and go into the kitchen.

"I heard what the meteorologist was reporting," I tell him as I pull two coffee cups from the cupboard. Rey's at the stove, assembling our plates.

"I'll fire up the fireplace tonight. It looks like we'll need to sleep in front of it tonight because those bedrooms are going to get extremely cold," he says as he turns toward the table. I pour coffee into our mugs. We both sit.

"I know. There are three cots in the closet. When I finish working, I'll pull them out and make them up." I put a forkful of egg into my mouth.

"That sounds uncomfortable," he says, and I chuckle.

"It does. Do you have a better idea?"

"I can pull the top mattress off each of our beds and place them near the fireplace."

"That sounds more comfortable and a lot warmer. Let's do that. I'll make them up." I take another bite of the egg. "Breakfast is really good, as usual"

"Thanks. I'm good at breakfast. I suck at all other meals," he says.

I laugh, and he stops eating.

"What?" I ask, still smiling. "Do I have something on my face?" I swipe at my mouth with my napkin.

"No. That laugh stuns me every time. I haven't heard you laugh in a very long time, and I love hearing it." He smiles. "It's a beautiful sound."

I can feel myself blushing. "Thank you. It feels good to do it again."

We finish our breakfast in silence. We share a glance occasionally. The sexual tension between us is palpable. When I'm done, I pick up my plate and take it to the sink. I place the dirty dishes in the sink and turn to Rey.

"Are you finished?" I ask him.

"Yes." I reach over and pick up his plate. "Thank you."

I wash the dishes and he refills his coffee cup. He takes a sip and puts the cup down. He starts drying and putting away the dishes. We work in silence but the glances between us are electric.

Once we're done, I go back to work, and Rey goes out to get firewood.

****

Later that day, when I finish working, I make up the beds. Rey picked up the firewood, brought the mattresses into the living room, and went on a grocery run. We don't need much. Tomorrow afternoon we're leaving for the wedding. We're leaving the day before the wedding, so we don't have to rush the day of. I'm grateful because I'm planning on getting my hair and nails done. My hair and nails are in desperate need of a professional touch.

I decide to start packing my bag and go into my bedroom. I pull out my small carry-on and start to pull clothes, fold them, and place them in the bag. I go to the dresser drawer and start rummaging through my underwear. I pull out a few pieces and put them into the bag. I grab another small bag and put the shoes I'll need into it. I hear the door open and put the bags in the closet.

I walk out of the bedroom as Rey walks into the kitchen.

"Hi," I say as I walk into the kitchen behind him. He places the bags on the counter and turns. He closes the space between us and places his arms around my waist. My arms come up around his neck of their own accord.

He holds me close for a minute. He pulls back a little so he can look into my eyes. It feels so perfect in his arms.

"Hi," he says, leaning down and placing his lips on mine. He pulls back and smiles. "All done with work?"

"Yes," I answer, and we reluctantly pull apart. We both head to the counter and unpack the groceries. "What do you want for dinner?"

"It doesn't bother me. I'll eat anything," he says. "Is there anything you want?"

I open the fridge and put the milk and eggs away. I notice the rest of the dough I made up for the flatbread. "How about pizza?"

"Sounds great but there aren't any pizza places around here." He's leaning against the counter now, watching me.

I laugh. "I mean I'll make us a pizza." I hand him a beer.

He takes it. "Thanks, and that sounds amazing!"

"Great! What do you like on your pizza?" I ask as I start placing the dough and cheese on the counter.

"Everything. I like my pizza loaded."

"That's easy." I pull out mushrooms, sausage, onions, olives, and peppers.

"I bought a movie to watch tonight," he says and takes a pull of his beer.

"How are we going to watch it? There isn't a DVD player here." I take the veggies to the sink to wash them. I pull out a bowl and turn on the water.

"I checked the TV, picked up a DVD player, and some movies," he says. "How can I help?"

"A movie sounds great. I haven't watched one in a very long time." I hand him the block of cheese. "Please grate."

"Yes, ma'am." I laugh as he starts on the cheese.

Chapter 13

Kat

An hour later, the pizza was made and eaten. Dishes were washed and put away. Now, I'm sitting on the couch looking through the movie selection while Rey hooks up the DVD player. He has great titles-*Dirty Dancing, Pretty Woman, Top Gun, Footloose,* and *Dear John.*

"You have great movies here. I've wanted to watch *Dear John*," I tell him.

"I guess we're watching *Dear John*." He looks at me with a big smile on his face.

"No, what do you want to watch?" I ask him.

"I've seen them all but *Dear John*. I know it's going to be a total chick flick, but a military man's worst nightmare. So, I'm curious about how they put it into a movie."

"Okay." I rip the wrapping off the movie and hand it to him. He pops the movie into the player and comes to sit next to me on the couch.

I'm sitting with my knees bent and my feet underneath me. My elbow of my left arm sits on the back of the couch. He sits so I face him. He places his hand on my knee and smiles at me. I lean a little closer and place my right hand on his forearm. He watches me do this, leans in, and gives me a quick kiss. He turns to the TV and presses play.

We watch the movie in silence. At times, I get emotional, and he places a comforting arm around me. It's a total chick flick but a great movie, nonetheless. By the time the movie ends, I'm leaning up against Rey and he has his arm across my shoulders.

"What did you think of the movie?" I ask.

"It was good. It was heartbreaking and extremely emotional but really good."

"I agree. I understand why she did what she did, but I don't agree with the way she did it." He turns to me.

"You would've told him the truth in the letter?" he asks me. He seems shocked by my response.

"Yes, I would've. She was doing something to help a friend and I think John would've understood. I'm not saying it wouldn't hurt him, but at least he would know she didn't give up on him." He has an odd expression on his face. He shakes his head.

"That's honorable, but what if John didn't want you to do it?"

"I don't know. I'm not in her shoes but I know I wouldn't have kept it from him or made him believe he wasn't loved," I explain.

"You're a very honorable person, Kat. I admire that. Most people would protect their hearts, yet you would put it on your sleeve." He smiles at me.

"I believe the truth is always best." I smile back. I stand up and walk into the kitchen. A minute later, I hand him a beer. He takes a pull of it, and I sip my water.

He walks over to the fireplace and places his beer on the mantle. He stacks the wood and starts the fire. He places the screen in front of it and turns to me.

"We should try to get some sleep. We have a long day tomorrow," he says.

Chapter 14

Kat

I'm lying in my bed, on my stomach, watching the fire when Rey comes out of the bathroom and walks toward his bed. I look up as he approaches. My mouth goes dry. He's climbing into his bed without a shirt and a pair of grey sweatpants. The muscles in his back ripple as he pulls the covers back and sits down. He's toned and beautifully muscular. Not too much and not too little. He's just perfect and extremely sexy. I turn away, but I know he noticed me looking. He lies on his side facing me. I look at him and smile. I pull the pillow up under my chin.

"So, tell me. What made you join the Army?" I ask.

His eyebrows go up and he nods. "Well, I went to college and took a few courses, but I couldn't figure out what I wanted to do. My head was all over the place. So, I decided to investigate the military. I walked into the recruiter's office, and we spoke for a long time. He showed me all the Army had to offer. I left the office and for a week I just kept thinking about it. I decided it was the right thing for me." He pauses. "I didn't have anything else. Plus, defending our country seemed right. I know our roots are Portuguese, but we were born and raised in the USA."

I nod. I completely understand what he's saying. "I'm glad you found happiness with your career. Thank you for fighting for our freedom. I can't even imagine what you've been through fighting in the war. When I found out you were in Iraq fighting, my heart dropped, and I was always trying to find out if you were okay."

He closes his eyes for a second and when he opens them, he's distant. It's as if he's back in Iraq. "It was, by far, the scariest thing I've ever been through. I saw things no one should ever see. The amount of death and destruction is indescribable. I had some therapy sessions for PTSD, but it never goes away. The nightmares will always be there, and the flashbacks happen occasionally."

"How did you get through it? How did you not give up?" I ask.

"Well, it's your job and you have colleagues counting on you. We're a family. We bonded in a way no one can understand unless you're going through what we did. You also think of your family and how much you want to see them again. You do your best to focus on the task at hand. When danger approaches, you do your best to stay safe, but it isn't something you can control. I keep pictures of everyone I love in my wallet. Every night, I would take them out and look at them. The pictures helped me focus. I believe those pictures got me through." He takes a deep breath and stands. I watch as he walks into his bedroom and comes back carrying his wallet. He sits on his bed and opens it. He pulls out the pictures and hands them to me. I sit up and take them from him. There's a picture of his mom, his dad, his brother, and…me. I stare at the picture and look at him. He's watching me very carefully.

"When was this picture taken?" I ask him, still staring at the picture. My hair fell around my face, and I had a huge smile on my face. It's a great picture. I look so young.

"At John's graduation party. My mom took that picture. She asked me to pick up the pictures she had dropped off for development. I went and looked through them before I left the store. I saw that picture and I couldn't stop looking at it. I cut it to fit my wallet and I've carried it with me ever since." He's staring at me, waiting for my reaction.

I look up at him. Tears fall down my face. "You've carried this picture around for almost fifteen years?"

"Yes, and it always makes me smile. I hoped and prayed you were happy. I knew my chances with you were gone but I always wanted happiness and love for you." He looks down at his feet and backs up at me. Tears still fall. I wipe them away and move off the bed. I kneel in front of him and place my hands on his.

"Thank you for always wanting happiness for me. I've always wanted the same for you. I've had my happiness, but I've had more sadness. That's just how life goes. I thought of you all the time and prayed you were safe. You were the one that got away and I always wondered if you were happy and if you had found love. I prayed you did." I smile at him through the tears. He places a hand on my cheek and wipes a tear away with his thumb.

"My one regret is not making you mine all those years ago," he says. He isn't smiling and is searching for something in my eyes. I can see the seriousness and the depth of his feelings in his eyes. I hope he can see how much I care about him.

"No regrets. We have a chance now," I say.

"Yes, we do and I'm not letting you go."

He kisses me then. His lips are soft and hot. It's a soft kiss. He moves his lips over mine slowly, but with slight pressure. He pulls away quickly and leans his forehead on mine.

"We should get some sleep," he says.

"You're right." I move away from him. I climb into bed, and he does the same. "Good night."

"Good night. Sleep well, sweetheart," he says, and I close my eyes.

Chapter 15

Kat

I can't sleep. I have no idea how long I've been laying here, unmoving. My mind won't shut off, as usual. But I'm not thinking of the usual stuff. I'm thinking of my family but not in the same way as I was a week ago. I have a little bit of guilt for deciding to move on but I'm not letting it consume me. I miss my family more than I can explain and I always will, but I can't let losing them take over my life anymore. I already missed out on five years.

But now, my thoughts are on Rey. I'm thinking about the picture he showed me tonight and the kiss we shared. We've shared a few kisses, but the kisses never go farther than the mere touching of lips. He's never tried to deepen the kiss. I haven't tried it either, but I don't know how to approach it. I guess I need to make the first move. Maybe that's what he's waiting for. He promised not to push me, and I'm so appreciative of that. But I want more. I want to move our relationship along. We finally have our chance and I'll admit a piece of my heart always belonged to him. I loved my husband so much and I gave him all I had. We had a great life and two beautiful children. I wouldn't have given it up for anything or anyone. Unfortunately, they have been taken from me and now I have a chance to be happy again. I want it so much. I feel so old and worn out from the last five years and I'm tired of feeling this way.

I open my eyes and find my phone. It's two in the morning. My thoughts have consumed me for the past three hours. I look at Rey. He's lying on his side, facing me, with his eyes closed. I move to the edge of my bed and stand. I stand there for a minute and take two deep breaths. His eyes open and he moves up onto his elbow.

"Are you okay?" he asks.

"I can't sleep."

"Are you cold?" He looks at the fireplace to make sure the fire is still going. He looks back at me.

"A little." I move toward his bed and sit on the edge.

I watch his face as he watches me. I take another deep breath and lie next to him. I lay on my side facing him. He freezes for a second and smiles. He brings the blanket up around us and lies down with his arm under his pillow. He drapes the other arm around me and his hand rests on the small of my back. I place one arm under my pillow and my other hand rests on the bed between us. I watch him for another second, then close my eyes.

****

I stretch as I wake up. I feel so cozy, and I don't want to open my eyes. I feel an arm tighten around my waist and I open my eyes. Rey's watching me. I smile at him.

"Good morning," I say.

"Good morning." He flashes me that sexy smile.

I look down at our bodies. We're still in the same position as last night, except my foot rests on top of his. I move it back to my side.

"Why did you move your foot?" he asks.

"I don't want you to be uncomfortable."

"I slept better than I've ever slept. I was having a hard time sleeping last night too until you came to lie beside me." He brings the hand around my waist up to brush a loose strand of hair off my face. He leans in and gives me a quick kiss.

"What time is it?" I ask, assuming I slept my normal three hours.

"Eight." My eyes go wide.

"What's wrong?"

"Absolutely nothing. I'm shocked. I haven't slept more than three hours a night for the past five years. But, with you next to me, I was able to sleep six hours," I say, watching his face.

"Now we know what was missing for both of us." He responds and pulls me close to him. He holds me like that for a few minutes. "Are you ready for the weekend?" he asks with his chin resting on my head.

"Yes, I just need to pack my toiletries. What time do you want to leave?" I ask as I breathe in his clean masculine scent.

"Whenever you want." I feel his hand move up and down my back.

"How about we get ready, go have breakfast, pick up the car, and head on our way?" I suggest. He pulls away to look at me.

"What about your writing?"

"I'm taking the weekend off. Plus, I'm ahead of the game, so I can."

"Let's do it!" he says, and we both move to get up at the same time. We both start laughing and head toward our bedrooms.

Chapter 16

Kat

Later that day, I'm standing in the lobby of the most gorgeous hotel while Rey checks us in. The drive was beautiful. The mountain views were breathtaking. Holding Rey's hand or his hand on my leg felt so good. Our connection never broke the whole way here. The hotel is fancy. I know Rey's spending a small fortune to stay at this hotel. I see a sign for a spa. I head to the concierge to get more information on their services.

"Hello, Miss. Can I help you?" he asks.

"Yes. I would like some information on the spa, please," I tell him.

"Sure. A minute." He picks up the phone. He gives someone a code. "A rep from the spa will be with you in a minute."

"Thank you."

A minute passes and an older lady in a suit comes out to greet me. She holds her hand out for me to shake. I shake it and she smiles.

"Hello, my name is Sara. I do the tours and scheduling for the spa. I was told you were interested in some services," she says.

"I'm Kat. I'm going to a wedding tomorrow. I would like a manicure, pedicure, and something with my hair."

"We can help. Do you have a few minutes for a tour?" she asks.

"Can you give me a minute?"

"Sure, dear," she says, and I walk over to Rey. I tell him what I'm doing and ask him if he can wait a few minutes for me.

"No problem, sweetheart. Take your time. I'll go have a beer at the bar while I wait," he says.

"Okay. I shouldn't take very long." I kiss his cheek and walk back toward Sara.

Sara shows me every corner of the spa. Once we're done with the tour, she shows me a brochure with their packages and the prices for individual services. She informs me that getting a package is significantly cheaper than getting individual services. She gets me a glass of water while I review their packages. I choose the package for a complete hair service, manicure, pedicure, massage, and two waxing services. I make the appointment and walk out of the spa. I go to the bar to find Rey sitting at the counter, beer in hand, watching the soccer game on TV. I walk up behind him and place a hand on his back. He turns and smiles at me.

"Hey. All set?" he asks.

"Yes. I made the appointment for first thing tomorrow morning. I've never done anything like this before, so I'm kind of excited." I smile at him.

"Great. I'm glad you're doing it. You deserve some pampering." He grabs my hand. "Do you want anything to drink?"

"Yes. Diet Coke, please." I sit on the barstool next to him. Rey orders my drink, and we sit and watch the game until our drinks are finished. The bartender hangs out with us and gives us a few tips on what to see while we're here.

Once we're done, Rey pays the bill and sends thanks to the bartender. They shake hands and we head up to our rooms. We get into the elevator and Rey presses the button for the tenth floor. He turns to me and grins. He holds my hand as we wait for the elevator to reach our floor. Sparks fly between us, but he doesn't make a move. Once there, we walk hand in hand to our doors. He hands me my room card and we stop in front of my room first.

"Mine is right next door. Let's make sure your room's okay," he says. I nod and put the card into the slot. The light turns green, and I open the door. Rey holds it open until I go through and follows me in. I turn on the lights and walk to the window. I pull back the curtains and see a magnificent pool view. No one is at the pool considering it's still very cold out. I turn back to Rey and smile at him.

"The room is beautiful. Thank you."

"You're very welcome." He walks over to me. "It's still early, so you can take a nap or just relax until dinner."

"That sounds great. What time do you want to go to dinner?"

"Seven?" he asks.

"Perfect."

"Great. I'll see you in a little while." He leans down, places his hand on my cheek, and kisses me. He lingers on my lips for a minute and pulls back. He looks into my eyes and smiles. He caresses my cheek with his thumb. He walks out of my room quickly. A second later, I hear his door close, and his TV turns on. I pick up my bag and pull out my book and cell phone. I walk to the bed and set the alarm on my phone. I lie on the bed and start reading.

Chapter 17

An hour later, I close the book and throw it on the bed next to me. I can't concentrate on what I'm reading. I've read and reread the same chapter three times. I keep thinking about Rey. He's been so kind and patient with me. He's been so sweet and gentle. I realize I'm so in love with him but I'm so afraid to tell him and lose him. *What if we start our life and something happens to us? I can't lose someone else. I'll lose my mind. I won't be able to recover from it and will probably die from the pain.* I've had feelings for Rey for so long and I'm excited and nervous about our relationship. We finally have our chance, and I can't let him go. *But why can't I just follow my heart? Why do I keep fighting it?* Tears fall down my face. I wipe my face and climb off the bed. I go into the bathroom and turn on the water in the tub. I unpack my toiletries while the tub fills. I undress and slip into the hot water. I close my eyes and think of Rey and all the possibilities around us.

****

Rey

I turn off the TV and close my eyes. I'm lying on the bed, thinking about Kat. I can't stop thinking about her. She's going to be the death of me. I love her and want her so bad, yet I don't want to push her. I don't want to pressure her, but I want to touch her all the damn time. I want to kiss her whenever I want. I want to give her the world, but we need to go at her pace. The last thing I want to do is freak her out. She's been through hell and back and I know she's terrified of losing me. I get it, but I want her. I need her. Okay, I need to regroup. She needs to call the shots. When she's ready, she'll tell me. Hopefully.

Oh man, these walls are thin. I can hear her moving around in her room and I would give anything to be lying like this in her room, just watching her. *Hold on, did I just hear the water turn on?* Oh crap. Now, I'm going to fantasize about her in the shower or the tub. I run my hand through my hair and grunt. My brain can't handle any more images. I'm aroused just looking at her and I'm picturing her in the shower, wet and soapy. I look at the clock. I still have two hours before dinner. I stand up and walk into the bathroom.

****

Two hours later, I'm knocking on Kat's door. I hear her walking to the door. A second later, the door opens. She looks fucking gorgeous. Everything this girl wears looks amazing on her. She's wearing black pants, a light blue button-down blouse, and black heels on her feet. Her hair is in a braid. She never wears her hair down. I wonder why. She has little makeup on, and her lips are slightly glossy. I want to devour that mouth, but I need to keep control.

key." She says with a small smile.

"Hi," I respond. "You ready?"

"Let me grab my purse." She walks to the small desk. I watch as she walks. She's got an amazing ass. So round and so perfect. I need to look away, so I look down at my shoes. A minute later, she's closing the door behind her.

We walk to the elevators. I press the button and turn to her.

"You look great," I say. She blushes and looks down.

"Thank you. You look nice, too."

I smile and grab her hand. The elevator door opens, and we step in. I press the button for the lobby. I know tonight's going to be a very nice evening.

Chapter 18

Kat

It's nine o'clock in the morning and I'm heading down to the salon. I have a nine-thirty appointment. It's going to take a while. I'm a little excited considering I've never done this. The package wasn't cheap, but I need to do this for the wedding and myself. My self-esteem needs a boost. Lately, when I look in the mirror, all I see are bags under my eyes, grey hairs, and pale skin. Honestly, I don't know how Rey hasn't run screaming from me. I see the looks other women give me when I'm with him. They look at him and look at me and are probably wondering why he's with me. He's gorgeous and I look like an old lady who doesn't care about my appearance. That stops today. I won't be vain about it, but my hair will not be grey anymore and I'll keep up with my eyebrows at least. As far as manicures and pedicures go, I may keep up with them too. Rey deserves a woman that takes care of herself. I'm low maintenance and won't change it, but Rey deserves for me to look good. Worrying about my appearance is exhausting and I only want to worry about it as limited as possible.

I walk out of the elevator and head to the salon's front desk. I'm greeted with a huge smile from the associate. I sign in at the clipboard and sit down.

"Ms. Rodrigues," she says. I stand and smile at her. "Please, follow me. Your stylist is ready for you."

I follow her to an empty salon chair, and she motions for me to sit down. A moment later, a young girl approaches and gives me a big smile. She has a short pixie cut that's purple. She's pale with very dark black eyeliner. She has an amazing smile and I instantly feel comfortable with her.

"Lisa, this is Ms. Rodrigues. She'll be your stylist today." The associate from the front introduces us. She smiles at both of us and goes back to the front desk.

Lisa holds out her hand to me. I take it and we shake. "Please, call me Kat."

"Great, Kat. It's very nice to meet you." Lisa says.

"You, too," I respond.

"What would you like done today?"

I quickly explain I need a color and cut. I also tell her I'm going to a wedding this afternoon and need my hair simply done. I tell her I want to wear my hair down.

"Perfect. I know just the color and cut I want to do. Once we're done with it, I'll blow dry your hair. After, I'll get a description of your dress and go from there. Sound good?"

"That sounds great. I'm also getting a manicure, pedicure, massage, and waxing today," I tell her.

"Good for you. Every girl deserves some pampering now and then," Lisa says and places her hand on my shoulder. "Would you like to discuss your color?"

"No. I trust you."

She leans down, got close to my ear, and says, "I promise it won't be purple."

We laugh, and she walks away to mix up my hair color.

****

Three hours later, I'm looking in the mirror and I can't believe it's me. My hair's a dark brown now, cut to my shoulders, and Lisa has straightened it with a flat iron. It's pin-straight and so shiny. I have a little color on my cheeks and my eyebrows are beautifully shaped. They bring out my eyes. Lisa decided to leave my hair completely down and put a rhinestone bobby pin to hold my hair back from my eyes on one side. It's simple yet very elegant. My manicure and pedicure were done while my hair was set with color and deep conditioning. My eyebrows, legs, and bikini areas are waxed. The massage was done before my hair was styled.

"What do you think?" Lisa asks. I look up at her and she looks nervous.

"I love it," I say as I look back into the mirror. "You did an amazing job." My eyes fill with tears and Lisa panics when she sees them.

"Oh, honey. Are you okay? If there's something you don't like, I'll fix it," she says as she hands me a tissue.

"No, Lisa. I love it. I wouldn't change anything."

"Then why the tears?" she asks.

"It's been a very ugly five years. Just a few days ago, I made a huge life-altering decision, and this is part of it. Today's the start of a new chapter in my life. For the first time in five years, I'm happy and excited." I tell her.

"I'm happy for you. I don't know anything about you, but from the moment you sat in my chair, I knew you were something special." Lisa says, and more tears fall down my face.

I stand and give her a tight hug. She hugs me back just as tightly. I thank her and go to the front desk to pay. I give Lisa her tip, another quick hug, and head back up to my room.

Chapter 19

Kat

The wedding starts at three this afternoon. Rey says we need to leave at two. As soon as I got back to my room, I walked right into the bathroom and started the water in the tub. My legs are waxed so it saves me some time. I take a bath to relax my nerves a little. I finish with my bath and put on a black lacy bra with a matching thong. I put on my robe and go to work on my make-up.

Twenty minutes later, I'm putting on my dress. Rey will be at the door in a few minutes. The dress is an ankle-length black dress that's form-fitting. It isn't tight but shows off my curves. It has a slit up to the thigh of my right leg. When I tried this dress on, I didn't think twice about buying it. It looked good and it was very comfortable. I put on a pair of peep-toe black pumps and put on the necklace and earrings. I stand in front of the full-length mirror outside the bathroom. Well, that's as good as it's going to get. There's a knock at the door.

****

Rey

The door opens, and I stop breathing. Kat looks stunning. My eyes travel down her body as I take her in. Her hair is loose and straight with a small strand of rhinestones on one side. Her blue-grey eyes pop with the dark brown hair color and the make-up. She's wearing a long black dress that accentuates those amazing curves of hers. She's wearing heels that show her toes. Her toenails have red nail polish and it's extremely sexy.

I suck in the air and let it out slowly. She stands there smiling at me with a slight blush on her cheeks.

"You look very handsome, Rey," she says.

"Th...Thank you," I respond. "You look...wow! There aren't any words."

"Thank you." She turns to grab her small handbag. She opens it and puts her lipstick in it. She walks back to me and that's when I notice the slit up to her thigh. I think I just stopped breathing. I grab onto the door jam. My knees go weak, and I'm afraid I'm going to drop to the floor. Her right leg peeks out from her dress, and I'm immediately aroused. I want that leg wrapped around me.

I move out of the way as she closes the door behind her. I put my hand out and she takes it as we walk to the elevator. I press the button and turn to her.

"You do look stunning." She blushes and gives me a small smile. "I'm going to have to keep you close to me. I don't want other guys to get any ideas."

"Thank you."

"You finally wore your hair down."

"I finally got it cut, styled, and colored," she says.

"I've been dying to run my hands through it." Her eyes have fire in them at my words. I take a deep breath as the elevator doors open.

I press the lobby button and the elevator starts moving. I abruptly press the STOP button and push her against the elevator wall. My hands are on her waist and her hands are on my forearms.

I place a kiss on her lips and pull away with my forehead to hers. She smiles.

"This is going to be a long night," I tell her. "You drive me insane on a regular day but today, in that dress, shit."

"I must admit you're driving me just as crazy. You look amazingly sexy," she whispers as her cheeks flush.

I kiss her again and step away from her. I press the STOP button again and the elevator continues its descent. I grab her hand and lace my fingers through hers. I look into her eyes and bring the back of her hand to my mouth. I kiss it and she blushes. I love it when she blushes.

"Tonight's going to be amazing."

"I agree," she says.

The elevator doors open, and we walk to the valet. I notice all the men in the lobby stop and look at Kat. Everything about her is gorgeous. Her hair, her body, her personality, her heart. She's perfect and my heart swells with so much love for her. Eat your heart out guys. She's all mine.

I hand the valet a card. A minute later, he appears with the car and stops right in front of us. He jumps out and opens the door for Kat. I move in front of him and help her into the car. I close the door and turn to the moron. I give him a dirty look and tip him.

"Thank you."

"Thank you, sir. Have a wonderful evening," he says and turns to go back to his post.

I walk around the front of the car and climb in. I smile at her and we're on our way.

Chapter 20

Kat

A little while later, I'm standing at a high table with Rey's parents. The ceremony was beautiful and now we're at the cocktail hour. Rey and Paul, Rey's father, went to the bar to get some drinks for me and Luisa.

"You look so beautiful, sweetheart," Luisa says, placing her hand on mine.

"Thank you. I love your dress. You look very pretty," I say, smiling at her.

"Thank you. How you've been?" she asks.

"I'm doing well. I'm slowly moving on," I answer. "Rey's helped me a lot."

"I'm happy to hear it. You deserve happiness. When I heard what happened, I just couldn't reach out to you. What could I say to you to make it better? Nothing. So, I prayed for you. I still pray for you." She has a genuine look on her face. I can feel tears swell in my eyes.

"I appreciate that." I try to blink away tears. No crying tonight.

"I'm extremely happy you and Rey are getting close," she says with a big smile. I can feel a blush come across my face.

"We are. We've decided to give a relationship a try. We've lost so many chances and we aren't going to let this chance go by," I tell her.

"I couldn't be happier to hear that." She brings me into a tight hug.

At that moment, Rey and Paul walk up. Both of them stand there, holding drinks, and watching us. When Luisa lets me go, she pats my cheek and smiles.

Paul clears his throat and we both look at them.

"Is everything okay?" Rey asks, handing me a glass of white wine.

"Yes, we were catching up," Luisa says, smiling at her son.

I take a sip of my wine and smile at Rey. He smiles back and takes a pull of his beer. He places a hand on the small of my back. The warmth spreads through me and immediately calms me. Just then, Uncle Manny and Aunt Lina walk up. They both have a glass of wine in their hands. Aunt Lina hugs Luisa and Uncle Manny shakes Paul and Rey's hands. Aunt Lina looks at me and holds out her arms. I walk over to her, and she pulls me into a tight hug.

"It's so nice to see you, my sweet girl!" She pulls away and looks me up and down. "You look beautiful!"

"Thank you. It's great to see you, too," I say, smiling at her.

Aunt Lina hugs Rey and Paul. She goes back to Luisa, and they begin chatting.

Uncle Manny's watching me with a sly smirk on his face. I smile at him and walk toward him. He hugs me tightly.

"Rey can't keep his eyes off you, and I certainly don't blame the boy," he whispers, smiling. I can feel my face get hot. I look at Rey and, sure enough, he's watching me.

"Thank you," I say and walk back to Rey. When I'm next to him, he places his hand on the small of my back yet again, and I feel a bolt of electricity run through my body. I love that he wants to touch me. I take a sip of my wine and try to keep up with the conversations. It's so difficult because all I want to do is wrap my arms around Rey and bury my face in his neck. He smells so good. It's a mix of soap and a woodsy-smelling cologne.

When I saw him in my room earlier, I had to remind myself to breathe. He's wearing a black suit with a blue shirt and a solid black tie. I've never seen a man look so hot in a suit. As soon as I saw him, I felt a surge of heat run through me. I wanted to pull him into my room, strip him naked, and have my way with him. Screw the wedding. Every time I look at him, it's all I want to do.

"You keep blushing and it's driving me insane," Rey whispers in my ear. There goes the heat in my face again. I look up at him and he takes a deep breath. He looks deep into my eyes, and we stay locked like that for a minute. Uncle Manny's voice breaks the spell.

"My master plan worked," he says. *Wait. What?* Rey and I both turn to look at him and I notice all four of them are watching us, grinning.

"What master plan?" Rey asks.

"Do you think both of you staying in my apartment is a coincidence?" he asks. "Kat asked me first, but when you called about staying there, I knew it was finally the time for the two of you to get this going." He has a sheepish grin on his face. He's so proud of himself. I can't believe he set us up. Rey and I assumed his old age made him forget he had rented me the apartment.

"What? You set us up?" Rey says with a shocked expression on his face.

"I sure did. By the looks of it, I'm happy I did." He winks at Rey. We look at each other and back at the four of them.

"Did the rest of you know about this?" Rey asks.

"Yes." The other three say in unison. The four of them start laughing. Rey and I look at each other. We smile and shake our heads.

"I'm so glad you did that," Rey says.

"Me too," I agree. Rey leans in and places a light kiss on my lips.

"Awww!" The four of them say. Rey and I laugh.

"Uncle Manny and the rest of you, thank you. Rey has been an enormous help to me. I appreciate you stepping in." I shake a finger at Uncle Manny. "No more setting me up. Got it?" He laughs and comes over to me. He hugs me. When he pulls away, he puts his hand on my face.

"You needed him, so I gave him a little push," he tells me.

I nod, and everyone starts laughing.

Chapter 21

Kat

A couple of hours later, Rey and I tore up the dance floor. We're having so much fun. I finally let my hair down and I'm having a great time. It's been at least six years since I danced like this. I forgot how much I love to dance. We've danced to everything that's been played. The DJ is on fire and plays everything but slow dances. He only played those for the bride and groom dance, the father-daughter dance, and the mother-son dance. The dinner was delicious. We're sitting with Rey's parents and cousins. The wedding cake has just been cut and dessert is being served.

I sit down at the table and Rey went to the bar to refill our drinks. I had one glass of wine during the cocktail hour and another glass during dinner. The rest of the time, I've been drinking Diet Coke or water.

"Kat, are you having a great time?" Aunt Lina asks me.

"I am. I haven't had this much fun in a very long time," I answer, smiling.

"That's wonderful, sweetheart. I've never seen Rey this happy. I can see the love in his eyes." She's smiling at me.

"He makes me very happy, too." I look down at my dessert plate.

Aunt Lina moves a little closer to me.

"It's okay to be happy, honey. You've spent enough time mourning. Your husband and children would want you to be happy. I won't even mention your parents. You know that" she tells me.

"I know. But I keep letting guilt stop me," I whisper.

"You have nothing to feel guilty about. You loved your husband, but he passed. You're young and deserve another chance at love. Rey's always loved you. Let him love you now." She put her arm around me. "You deserve this, and you deserve him."

"I love him very much. I've always loved Rey, but life didn't bring us together until now. I won't let him go," I say.

"Good girl!" She winks at me.

I laugh and hug her. "Thank you."

"You're very welcome." She stands. "I need to go find my husband and go dance."

I laugh and watch her walk away, leaving me alone at the table. I take a bite of cake and feel a hand on my shoulder. I know immediately it's Rey. The electricity coming from his hand shoots through my whole body. He places a Diet Coke and a beer down in front of me and leans down to whisper in my ear.

"I'll be right back," he says, and I nod. He walks toward the DJ. I watch him. Damn that man has an amazing ass. He says something to the DJ, and he nods. He heads back toward me with a smile on his face. He sits next to me. *What's he up to?*

"Are you having a good time?" he asks, smiling at me.

"Yes. I haven't had this much fun in a very long time. Thank you for asking me to come." I take another bite of cake. He picks up his beer and drinks.

"I'm over the moon you came with me, baby. I don't want this night to end."

Just then, the music stops, and the DJ speaks. "The next song is a dedication to Kat from Rey." I look at Rey and he's watching me. He puts his hand out and stands. The song 'Open Arms' by Journey starts to play.

"Dance with me?" he asks, and I place my hand in his. He walks back to the dance floor and never breaks eye contact with me.

He places both arms around me and I bring my hands up to the back of his neck. I place one hand on the back of his neck and the other hand goes into his hair. I get as close to him as possible. Our bodies mold together, and our faces are touching. He's singing to me. I close my eyes and tears begin to fall. I love him so much and I'm going to tell him tonight. I can't wait any longer to be in this man's arms.

For the first time since Rey stepped into my life, I don't feel any guilt. I'm happy, and my heart's exploding with love for him. He's my whole world now and I'll make sure he knows it from now on. No more holding back. I'm so tired of being alone and feeling guilty.

I open my eyes to see the bride and groom and other couples have joined us. I smile at the bride and groom. I pull my face from Rey to look him in the eyes. He stares at me. I lick my lips and bring his mouth to mine. I swipe my tongue along his bottom lip, and I hear him groan. He pulls away and looks at me. He must see what he needs in my eyes. He slams his mouth to mine and our lips meet again. This time, we deepen the kiss. Our tongues meet and move together for the first time. We explore each other thoroughly. It's an amazing kiss. When we pull away, we're breathless. We didn't notice the song ended, and the next song had started.

"Let's go outside for a minute," I say. He nods, and we walk out to the balcony. I turn to him.

"That kiss was amazing," he says. "I've never experienced a kiss like that."

"Me neither and, yes, it was. Thank you for the song dedication. One of my favorite songs and fitting to our situation," I tell him. "I asked you to come out here because I need to tell you something extremely important."

His face falls and he looks as if he just got punched in the stomach. I place both my hands on either side of his face and our eyes lock.

"I love you, baby. So much. You're my world and I'm never going to let you go." I see a single tear fall down his face. Surprisingly, I don't cry. I want to shout from the rooftops how much I love this man.

"I love you too. I feel the same way. My heart bursts when I see you. I can't wait to see what life has in store for us."

"Me too, love, me too."

"You've just made me the happiest man," he says. "I think I've got the groom topped."

I laugh, and he smiles at me.

He places his hand on the back of my neck and brings my mouth to his. We kiss again. I don't know how long we kiss, and I honestly don't care. I'm finally with the man of my dreams.

Chapter 22

Kat

It's one in the morning when we head back to our hotel. I rest my head back on the headrest and close my eyes. I'm tired and energized all at once. Tonight's been such a magical night and I'll never forget it. Rey showed me what it's like to have fun again. He showed me how to feel alive. I've never felt the way I'm feeling right now. It's more than happy. It's contentment, excitement, and so much love. I feel like my heart's going to burst right out of my chest with how full it is. I can't believe Rey's with me. After all these years, we're finally together.

I feel Rey's hand cover mine and I smile. I turn my hand and lace my fingers through his. The warmth from his hand sends heat up my arm.

"Are you okay, baby?" he asks. I open my eyes and look at him. He quickly glances at me. I love when he calls me that.

"Yes, I was just thinking of tonight. I've had such a great time. I'll never forget it. Thank you. Thanks for all of it."

"I need to be thanking you. You've made every dream I've had come true tonight. I knew we would have a good time, but I never expected what was happening," he says.

I lean my head back again. I close my eyes and replay the night again.

"Are you tired, sweetheart?" he asks.

"Yes, but I'm energized at the same time."

We pull into the hotel and the valet walks up to the car. Rey steps out and the valet opens the car door for me. I step out and Rey holds out his hand. I take it and we walk into the hotel and straight to the elevators. He presses the up button and looks at me.

"What time do you want to head back tomorrow?" he asks.

"There's no rush. After breakfast should be okay."

"Sounds perfect." The elevator doors open. We step in and Rey presses the button for the tenth floor.

As soon as the doors close, Rey faces me and places his hands on my waist. He pulls me in close to him and kisses me so deeply. My hands rest on his chest as I melt into him. This man is a phenomenal kisser. Geez, my knees are weak and I'm not quite sure I can walk to my room. We pull apart as the doors open.

I step off the elevators in front of Rey slowly to be sure my legs will hold me. He follows me to my door, and I take the key card out of my clutch. I insert the card and open the door. I walk in, throw my clutch on the small table, and lean against the open door. I smile at Rey, and he comes closer.

"Good night, love. Sleep well," he says and kisses me gently. My hands come to rest on either side of his face. We pull apart and I look into his eyes.

"Stay with me," I say. He blinks as if he's trying to decipher if what I said was real. I just watch his reaction.

"Are you sure? There's no rush. I'm not going anywhere, and I'll wait as long as you need it. I don't want you to have any regrets." I place my finger over his lips, and he stops talking.

"Baby, I love you and there's nothing more I want than to make love to you. Don't you think we've waited long enough for each other?" The fire in his eyes causes butterflies to take flight in my belly. He swallows hard. He walks into the room and closes the door with his foot as his lips land on mine.

****

I step out of my shoes and Rey watches every move I make. I smile and walk over to him. He looks into my eyes.

"I love you," he says.

"I love you. There are a few things we need to talk about before we do this," I say.

"Okay," he says and leads me over to the couch by the window. We sit, and I turn a little to face him. He's patiently waiting for me to start.

"I believe in full disclosure. I also don't want to take something special away from you. I want a life with you, but I also want to be honest with you," I tell him. "You need to know what you're giving up being with me. I never want you to make any sacrifices to be with me."

"You're scaring me."

"No. It's not something to be scared about but it could change your plans for the future." I give him a weak smile and take a deep breath. He picks up my hand and holds it.

"You can tell me anything. I'm not going anywhere." I nod and continue.

"Don't make any decisions until you've heard what I need to tell you." I take a deep breath and continue. "During the accident, my uterus was punctured. It was punctured so badly that the doctors had to perform an emergency hysterectomy. I can't have any more children."

"Oh, wow. Have you had any complications from it?" He asks. I look at him, dumbfounded. I just told him I couldn't have children and he wants to know if I've had any complications from it.

"No. I just have a scar on my lower abdomen," I say.

"Well, thank god."

"Rey, did you hear me? I can't have children. I'll never be able to give you a child." I say as a tear falls down my cheek. He wipes the tear from my cheek with his finger.

"Do you think I would walk away from you because of that?"

"Yes, you're wonderful with children and I would assume having children is something you want." I can't believe he's so calm about this. He doesn't seem phased by my admission.

"I've always pictured having children, but I've also pictured you by my side. I don't want anything if I can't have you. This is not a deal-breaker. I love you and nothing will stop me from loving you. What happened to you was the most tragic thing that could've happened. I don't know how you made it through all of it, but I'm so grateful you're here with me. It saddens me you can't have any more children, but it doesn't change how I feel about you." Tears continue to fall down my face as I listen to him. "I know losing your children broke you and I would never ask you to go through that again. I just want you."

"So, you never expected to have children with me, regardless?" I ask.

"No, I didn't. I would never expect you to have more children. I have plenty of cousins and friends with kids and I'll enjoy them."

"Thank you for being so understanding." I wipe the tears from my face. He sits forward and takes me into his arms. I rest my head on his chest and his chin rests on the top of my head.

"I have everything I want and need right here." He strokes my head and runs his fingers through my hair.

Chapter 23

Kat

I pull away from Rey and look at him. He puts a hand under my chin and pulls me to him. He kisses me deeply and passionately. My hands come up and into his hair. His hands come around my back. I break the kiss and stand. He tries to stand but I place my hand on his chest. I take a step back and smile. I reach behind me and pull the zipper down. I reach up to my shoulders and pull down the straps. The dress falls to the floor and puddles at my feet. I step away from the dress and bend down to pick it up. When I stand back up, Rey sucks in a breath. I look at him as he takes my body in. He's devouring me with his eyes. He takes a step toward me.

"You're beautiful," he whispers. He grabs me and crushes me onto his body. He kisses me hard. He pulls back and we're both breathing hard. "I want you so bad."

"I'm all yours, baby," I tell him. I start unbuttoning his shirt. My hands feel the muscles on his chest. I suck in a breath. Oh my. This man has muscles I never knew existed. I push the shirt off his shoulders, and it falls to the floor. He's magnificent. So sexy and I can't wait to feel all of him. I'm so aroused. He can't touch me soon enough. Every part of this man turns me on.

Rey turns me around and unclasps my bra. It immediately loosens around my breasts, and he kisses my shoulders as he pulls the straps down my arms. The bra falls to the floor. He turns me back around and bends down to take a breast into his mouth. I feel an immediate rush in my belly and moan. It feels so good. I close my eyes and savor the feeling.

"That feels amazing," I whisper.

"I'm about to lose it, sweetheart," he says and continues with my breasts.

I reach down and place my hands on each side of his face. He looks up at me and I gently pull him up to my lips. I kiss him deeply and his arms come around me. He holds me so tightly. He pulls away from my lips and we're both breathing hard. He leans his forehead to mine.

"Are you okay?" I ask him as he closes his eyes.

"I'm trying to go slow and savor our first time, but it's taking everything out of me not to lose control," he says and takes a deep breath.

"Look at me." He looks me in the eyes. "It doesn't matter if you go fast or slow. It's you and me. We'll have many more times together." I wink at him. "We've waited a long time to be together. I'm just as desperate as you are."

"You never cease to amaze me, sweetheart." He links his fingers in my thong and pushes them down my legs. I step out of them. I stand before him completely naked. "Unbelievably beautiful."

He pushes me back onto the bed. I crawl back to allow him room. He pushes his pants and boxer briefs off and climbs onto the bed next to me. I watch him, and my eyes go wide when I see him naked. He's so perfect, sexy as hell, and huge. I want him so bad but I'm nervous. I still can't believe Rey's lying here with me. I feel the anticipation building in my belly.

He kisses me hard and deep as his hand travel up and down my hip and thigh. He kisses my neck, my chest, and my stomach. He comes back up to my lips and moves so he's in between my legs. His warmth on me makes me feel safe. He smiles down at me. "You're so sexy, baby."

I smile at him and move my hips.

"I'm not going to last long. I have the woman of my dreams in my arms, and I don't need a condom. I apologize in advance, but I promise I'll make it up to you," he says and comes down to me.

I laugh. "It's going to be amazing. It already has been, and I can't wait for more."

We kiss, and my hands caress up and down his back. He groans and goes down to my breasts. I feel his mouth take a nipple and arch my back. I feel his fingers touch my core and I whimper with pleasure.

"You're so wet, baby," he pants.

He positions himself and enters me slowly. I close my eyes as I feel him. He feels so good and I almost came from the initial sensation. I know I'm going to cum fast and hard because I'm finally making love to Rey.

When he's all the way in, he goes still. I open my eyes to see him watching me.

"You feel fucking amazing." He begins moving slowly, at first. His thrusts become more hurried, almost frenzied. Within a minute, I'm shattering beneath him. I look into his eyes as my orgasm hits me hard. He's moving faster now, and I can feel another build-up. He moves harder and faster and suddenly we're crying out each other's names as we explode into each other. He collapses on top of me. I wrap my arms and legs around him as we try to catch our breath. I know at this moment our love will always be this explosive. My heart swells with love for this incredible man. I'm finally happy and holding the man of my dreams in my arms. I'm never letting go.

Chapter 24

Kat

Rey shifts and brings his head up. His hands are in my hair, and he smiles at me. "Making love to you has been the most incredible experience of my life."

"Same for me. I didn't know it could be like that," I say and his smile fades.

"What do you mean?" he asks. We're still linked together in every possible way. I love the feeling of him on me like this. I feel so safe and loved.

"As you know, I've only been with one man. I loved my husband and sex was good but not anything like what I just experienced with you. My mind, my body and my heart were all experiencing it," I confess. "You make me feel safe and wanted."

"Baby, I promise you I'll always make sure you're safe. I've wanted you for so long and I'll always want you. Every part of me made love to you and I always will. It's never been this way for me either." He kisses me slowly and deeply.

"I love you," he says.

"I love you."

He shifts, and I release my hold on him. He rolls off me and stands. He reaches for me. "Come on."

I sit up. "Where?"

"We're going to take a shower." He smiles wide and I can't help but giggle. I jump up and run into the bathroom. He starts laughing and chases me into the bathroom.

****

An hour later, we're climbing back into bed. He lies on his back, and I curl into his side. My hand comes to rest on his stomach. I take a deep breath and feel Rey's arm come around me. His other hand rests on mine on his stomach. I smile and think of the past hour. We made love in the shower twice. We washed each other and now we're laying in bed, spent and satisfied.

He kisses the top of my head. "Sleep, baby." I smile and close my eyes.

****

Rey

I open my eyes. I look down and notice neither of us has moved. I look at Kat's face. She's sleeping so soundly. I smile and thank God this isn't a dream. For a while there, I thought this was all a dream and I didn't want to wake up. I tighten my arms around her. Her head moves but she doesn't wake up. I kiss her forehead. I love her so much. This woman's amazing. I'm so thankful I'm getting a chance with her.

I look over at the clock and see it's eleven. It was four in the morning when we finally got into bed. We slept for seven hours, yet it feels like I just closed my eyes. *Wait. Kat's still sleeping.* I smile down at her. I close my eyes and memories from earlier this morning flood my mind. Making love to her was completely mind-blowing. I've had other women, but no one compares to her. She's the only woman I ever want to make love to for the rest of my life. She's the only woman I'll ever want. She's completely ruined me for anyone else.

I feel Kat move and look down at her. She stretches against me, and I can feel my arousal growing. A small whimper comes from her mouth as she stretches. She opens her eyes and looks at me. She brings her hand up to my face.

"I wasn't dreaming right?" she asks.

"No, baby. You weren't." I lean down to kiss her, but she pulls away quickly.

"I have to brush my teeth," she says, and I laugh.

"Come here." I kiss her again. "I want a kiss from you as soon as we wake up every single morning for the rest of our lives."

She laughs. "Yes, sir." She kisses me again and I feel her push me onto my back. She straddles me. She sinks into me, and I moan. She looks down at me and her face reddens. "Is this, okay?" she asks.

"It's perfect, baby. I want to stay like this forever."

Chapter 25

Kat

Rey and I are walking from the elevators to the front door of the hotel when I hear my name called. I turn around and see Lisa running towards me. I smile when I see her. Even though I only met her yesterday, I like her and wish she lived in the states. We could be good friends.

"Are you leaving already?" she asks as she approaches me.

"Yes, we're heading back now." She comes toward me with her arms open wide. I lean in and hug her tight.

"Please come visit me the next time you're in town. I feel some sort of connection to you and I would like to remain friends," she says.

"Me too and you can count on it. Let me give you my information so we can keep in touch." We pull apart and I reach into my purse. I pull out a business card with my phone number and email on it. "Please email me." I smile at her.

"You got it. I'm so glad I met you." Her eyes travel to Rey, and she smiles. "Is this him?"

"Yes, it is. Rey, this is Lisa. Lisa, this is Rey. Lisa performed her magic on me yesterday when she did my hair," I tell him.

Rey smiles and extends his hand. "It's nice to meet you." She takes his hand, and they shake.

"It's nice to meet you, too. Take care of my girl. She deserves it."

I feel tears swell in my eyes as I look at her. She takes my hand. "Have a safe trip and I'll email you later."

"Thank you, Lisa." She nods her head. She walks away as Rey, and I continue toward the door. It suddenly hits me that Rey and I only have two more weeks together. Panic sets in. *What are we going to do after that?* I can't and refuse to lose him.

"Sweetheart, are you okay?" Rey asks. He looks so confused.

"What?"

"You just went pale, and you look like you're a million miles away." He takes my hand in his. The gesture is comforting but my stomach's turned.

"We have some important things to talk about on the drive back," I say. "It just hit me, and we need to figure some things out."

He nods his head, and I can see the panic in his eyes. The valet pulls the car up and opens the trunk. Rey puts the bags in the car, and we climb in. He tips the valet and we're on our way. Rey points to a small cooler behind his seat.

"There's water in there," he says and smiles weakly. "You look like you could use some. You still look so pale."

I reach into the cooler. I pull out two bottles of water and place one in the cupholder. I open the other and take a drink. Rey's giving me time to collect my thoughts. I turn in my seat a little, so I'm facing him. He glances at me.

"Saying goodbye to Lisa made me realize we only have two weeks left together," I say quickly. He nods and waits for me to continue. "It scared the crap out of me. We haven't discussed anything, and I have a million thoughts going through my head." I watch his reaction and he takes a deep breath.

"It hit me too but I'm not leaving you. We'll figure this out. I'm not going anywhere. I can promise you that. We might have to be separated every so often so things can be sorted out but that's the extent of us being apart."

"Where do you report after your time off is up?" I ask.

"I have to go back to Germany for two more months. It'll be Virginia, North Carolina, or California for two more years. Then, I can choose where I want to be." He responds with a glance at me. I'm sure he can see the wheels spinning in my head. My brain did a complete inventory of everything I have back home and instantly, I know I'm making the right one. I become excited and nervous at the same time. I'm excited for the next chapter in our lives but nervous because I'm not sure if Rey's going to agree. I must've taken too long to say something because Rey's pulling off the road and into a gas station. He pulls into a parking space and turns to face me.

"What are you thinking, baby?" The desperation in his voice shocks me. He looks so panicked.

"I'm thinking a lot of things and I'm hoping you'll agree with me." I take a deep breath.

"Tell me because I have no idea how to sort things out. I could never ask you to live in my world. Military life is difficult and constantly on the move. The good thing is we only have to deal with it for two more years and then I can be in a permanent place," he says so fast.

"You mean WE can be in a permanent place." I smile at him, and he stares at me. I continue. "When we get back to the apartment, I'm going to list my house and try to get it sold as soon as possible. I have the type of career where I can be anywhere. I only need a computer and a reliable internet connection."

"What are you saying?" I can see how surprised he is by the words coming out of my mouth. He watches me intently.

"I'm saying I'm going with you wherever you go if that's what you want." He runs a hand over his face and looks at me. "I know you're stuck but I'm not. I'm flexible."

"Are you serious?" he asks.

"Yes, I am." I'm starting to get scared because he's acting like he isn't happy about what I said. "If it isn't what you want…" He grabs my face and kisses me.

"I love you," he whispers.

"I love you, too, but I'm confused. Are you happy about what I said?" I'm staring at him and that's when I see it. The love in his eyes tells me everything I need to know.

"I'm over the moon, baby. I was expecting to do a lot of traveling until I could settle in one place. I, of course, would settle next to you once the time came. I was so scared to talk to you about this. I didn't want to pressure you or make you change your life for me. I was also so scared you would tell me to take a hike since I wouldn't be able to be with you all the time."

I smile at him. "Sorry but you're stuck with me." He laughs and pulls me to him. He kisses me feverishly this time.

"Being stuck with you is the only way I want to be," he says. "Tell me the specifics and let's figure it all out while we drive." He straightens in his seat and pulls back onto the highway. I reach into my purse and pull out a pen and paper.

The whole way back to the apartment, we talk about how to handle things and I take notes. We had a complete game plan by the time we got back.

Chapter 26

Kat

I unlock the apartment door and open the door wide so Rey can step in. He's holding both bags. He refused to let me carry one of the bags. He's such a gentleman. He's always been such a gentleman. I smile as I remember when he first opened the door for me. I remember heat forming in my cheeks as I walked through the door and thanked him. He had that sexy smile on his face. I just wanted to run into his arms and kiss him but, of course, I hadn't.

He steps into the apartment. I close the door behind us and notice he goes straight to our bedrooms. I walk into the kitchen and pull out a beer and a Diet Coke from the fridge. I'm opening the beer when I feel him come behind me. His arms come around my waist and I lean into him. I close my eyes and enjoy the feel of him. He feels so good and smells fantastic. He kisses the top of my head.

I raise the beer up. He takes it and takes a long pull from it.

"My girl in my arms and a cold beer. There's nothing better than that," he says, and I laugh. I take a sip of my soda and turn around. I place my head on his chest and my arms go around his waist. I hug him tightly and listen to his heartbeat. I could stay like this forever. The sound of his heart calms me and brings me such peace.

I pull back and look up at him. I bring my hand up to his neck and pull him to me. I kiss him hard and deep. I pour all of me into the kiss. I hear the beer hit the floor as Rey picks me up. He carries me to the couch. I smile, but don't pull away from his lips. He sits down, and I straddle his lap. He kisses me again and I can feel his hands going under the hem of my shirt. He's caressing my back and making me crazy for him. I break the kiss and push his shirt up and over his head. I start to kiss his chest. This man is so sexy and tastes so damn good. I'll never get tired of looking at him or feeling him. He turns me on so much. I undo the button of his jeans and continue kissing a path down his chest and stomach.

Rey tugs at my shirt and I sit up. I bring my arms up and he pulls off my shirt. His eyes go to my breasts and a sexy smile appears. He licks his lips and kisses my neck. He continues to kiss down to my stomach. He unclasps my bra and throws it on the floor. He starts fondling and kissing my breasts.

"That feels so good," I whisper in his ear.

He looks up at me and shifts to lay me down on the couch. He undoes the button and fly off his jeans and pushes them down. He pulls off my sneakers and my jeans follow his. I'm laying here in nothing but my thong. He stares down at me.

"You're so sexy, baby. I want you so bad."

I reach for him, and he comes down above me. His body and mouth mold to mine. His warmth enveloped me and there's no place on earth I would rather be. My hands travel through his hair and down his back. I cup his ass and he jumps.

"Are you okay?" I ask him, trying not to laugh.

"Yes, your touch does things to me I can't explain."

"I know exactly what you mean," I say, and he smiles. He stands and removes his boxers. He stands in front of me naked. I take him in inch by inch, and I still can't believe he's mine.

Rey comes back to me and kisses me gently. He pulls away slowly and looks into my eyes. His hand cups my cheek. "I love you so much. I can't believe you're with me. Thank you for taking a chance on us."

"I should be the one thanking you for putting up with my baggage. You're an amazing man and I'm a lucky girl. I love you and I'll always love you," I say.

His mouth comes to mine, and he slowly enters me. We both moan at the contact. He feels good. I'll never get enough of this man. The feelings Rey brings out of me can't be explained. He makes my heart swell and my body crazy for his touch. He breaks our kiss and begins to move slowly. The pace gets faster and faster and before we know it, we're both screaming each other's names.

Chapter 27

Kat

A week later, our plan is in full swing. My house has been put on the market. My realtor reassures me the house will sell quickly. I'm hoping it will since I don't want to be away from Rey for too long. I'm almost done with the first draft of my new novel. I can't take the smile off my face. I think of my family a few times a day, but I don't feel any guilt anymore. I miss them like crazy and often cry. I know I'll never fully get over the loss.

When I'm done working, Rey and I go sightseeing, take long walks on the beach, and shop. Every night, we fall asleep in each other's arms after making love. We enjoy every minute we have together because we know we'll be apart for an unknown amount of time. Our love grows stronger with every day that passes. There isn't anything I wouldn't do for him. He's my whole world. I would lay down my life for him.

I close my laptop and take a deep breath. Rey's sitting on the couch. He's reading the newspaper and looks up.

"Are you okay?" he asks.

"Yes. It was a sigh of relief. I finished the first draft of the book. Tomorrow, I print it and start editing. I have about two weeks until completion," I tell him.

"That's awesome and you're way ahead of schedule."

"Yep, and I also have ideas for the next three books I want to write."

He puts the newspaper down and gets up. He sits in the chair next to me. "I'm so proud of you." He kisses me.

"Thank you."

"Let's go dancing tonight at the casino."

"Sounds like a plan."

****

We dance the night away. We dance to everything that's played by the DJ. Rey's an amazing dancer and I love dancing with him. He moves so gracefully. The music changes and 'Save the Last Dance for Me by Michael Bublé starts to play. He takes my hand and twirls me around the dance floor. We fall into step so easily. Before I know it, no one is dancing but the two of us and everyone is watching us.

As soon as that song ends, 'Masterpiece' by Atlantic Starr starts to play. Rey pulls me close. His arm comes around my waist and he takes my hand. He brings it to his mouth, kisses it, and holds it close to his heart. My other hand rests on his bicep. We're cheek to cheek. I lose myself in this dance. It's such a beautiful song. I turn my face and kiss his cheek. I look at him and he stares into my eyes.

"You're so beautiful," he whispers.

"Thank you." I give him a small smile.

He brings his cheek back to mine. Tears swell in my eyes. I'm going to miss him so much. Being apart from him is going to shatter me. We've grown so close in such a short amount of time. I can be myself and he doesn't judge me or tell me I need to forget about my family. He understands me and what I went through. He understands I'll never get over what happened, and he lets me grieve. Every part of me is in love with him.

The song ends, and he leads me outside. The back of the casino overlooks the ocean. It's breathtaking. We're on the second floor and the breeze feels so good on my skin. He leads me to the railing and we both look out toward the water.

"What a beautiful view," I say, and he nods in agreement.

"It sure is." He looks at me and I smile. He makes my insides turn into jelly when he smiles at me like that. I've never reacted to someone as much as I react to him. Every part of me wants this man.

"You've been so distant tonight," he says. "We dance great together. You're my match in so many ways but it seems like something's weighing on your mind."

"I love dancing with you. I love doing everything with you. But you're right. I've been thinking about how much I'm going to miss you. I don't like not knowing when we're going to be together again." I face him.

"I feel the same way, but I also know we have to get through this little bump to never be apart again. I'll do whatever it takes to quickly get through this part."

"I know." I look back out at the water.

He comes toward me and wraps his arms around me. I bring my arms up and link them behind his head. He kisses me slowly and deeply. I melt into him. He explores every inch of my mouth and I do the same. He pours so much love into the kiss. This kiss tells me we can get through anything. Our love is strong, and I need to believe in it. We break our kiss, and he rests his forehead on mine.

"I love you."

"I love you," I say and take his hand. "The dance floor is calling us." I can't dwell on it because my mind will wander to ridiculous places. Just like Rey says, this is a bump in the road to be joined forever. Whatever it takes.

He smiles and follows me back into the club.

Chapter 28

Rey

I hold Kat's hand as I walk her to security at the airport. This month has flown by. I can see her fighting tears. She's been fighting them for the past hour. This is so fucking hard. I've been fighting my tears, as girly as it sounds. I don't want her to leave my side but, for it to happen, we have to go through this. She has to take care of things so we can be together. Saying goodbye to her is slowly killing me. In the end, we'll be okay, and she'll never be away from me again.

She looks at the security line and then down at her ID and boarding pass. I close my eyes and take a deep breath. I place my finger under her chin and bring her eyes to mine.

"Nothing changes," I say as she stares into my eyes. "We won't be apart for long."

"We're still apart, whether it's for a long or short time. It's killing me." Tears roll down her face and it shreds my heart into a million pieces.

She throws her arms around my waist and hugs me tightly. I hug her back just as tightly and kiss the top of her head. I rest my chin on her head and we stay like this for a few minutes.

She pulls away and wipes her face. "I guess I should get in line."

"Yeah," I say, and she looks up at me. I place both my hands on her face and kiss her.

"I love you, baby. I miss you already. Have a safe flight and call me when you get there, please," I tell her as tears keep falling down her cheeks.

"I will, and I miss you already, too. I love you so much. Please don't forget it," she says. I nod my head and I feel a tear roll down my cheek. I quickly wipe it away. She reaches up and kisses me quickly. She turns and walks into the security line.

I watch her until she goes completely through security. She turns and gives me a small wave. She hasn't stopped crying and it's killing me. I wait until I can't see her anymore and let the tears fall. I don't care who's watching me. The love of my life has left my side for an unknown time and my heart can't handle it. We've been apart way too long to be apart again.

****

A few hours later, I have the apartment completely cleaned and I'm packed. I'm leaving in the morning and mailing the keys to Uncle Manny. I called him earlier to thank him and he said he had spoken to Kat before she boarded the plane. She called him to thank him as well. I walk to the balcony and make sure my cell phone has a strong signal. I stand and pace back and forth. She should be calling any minute now. How am I going to get through this? It's only been a few hours and I feel like I'm already losing my mind.

I sit down, place my elbows on my knees, and run my hands through my hair. I miss her like crazy. I have no idea how I'm going to deal with not being with her. The phone rings.

"Hello."

"Hi, sweetheart." I smile when I hear her voice. "I just landed."

"I'm so glad you're safe. How was the flight?"

"It was good. I worked on my edits." She sounds so sad.

"I miss you so much. I feel like I'm going crazy," I whisper.

"Me too," she says, and I hear her sniffle. "I'm about to step off the plane."

"Ok. Get home safely. I'm going to try to get some sleep. My flight's early, and I'll call you when I get to Germany."

"Ok, baby. Be safe. I love you, Rey."

"I love you, too." She hangs up.

I stand and walk into the apartment. I close the balcony door and lock it. I turn off the lights and walk into what was Kat's bedroom. I undress down to my boxers and climb into bed. I lay my head on her pillow. It smells like her. I close my eyes and think about all the times I made love to her and wonder when I would be able to be with her again. Eventually, I fall asleep and dream of my beauty.

Chapter 29

Kat

Two weeks have gone by and I finally get the call I've been waiting for.

"Hi, Julia," I answer my cell phone.

"Hi, Kat. I got an offer on your house," she says.

"That's great!" I jump out of my chair.

"The offer is for your asking price. The buyer also wants all furnishings and is offering an additional fifteen thousand dollars for it," Julia tells me.

"That's an amazing offer and, of course, I'll take it."

"The paperwork will be in your email within the hour. It's a cash buyer so closing will be fast."

"That's amazing! Thank you, Julia. I'll get the paperwork back to you immediately."

"You're welcome." We hang up.

I place the phone down on my desk and switch to my email on my laptop. I type up an email to Rey letting him know about the offer.

For the last week, Rey's been working at the American Embassy and has been out of commission with the public. The only way to communicate with him is through email. I haven't heard from him in two days and I'm starting to worry. He did warn me this assignment would limit his ability to respond every day. So, I take a deep breath and pray I hear from him soon. It's killing me not knowing if he's okay.

****

A week later, closing happens and I'm all packed up to go. I sold everything but my clothes. I've only received one email back from Rey congratulating me on the offer and I haven't heard from him since. I have a bad feeling something's wrong. I try to shake it, but it keeps creeping up on me.

My flight to Germany is leaving at three tomorrow afternoon. I'm so excited to finally see Rey, but he still hasn't told me where to go or if he would be picking me up. I check my phone again to see if I've received an email. I didn't.

It's six o'clock in the evening and I decide to sit down and do some writing. I'm halfway through the next chapter when a knock comes on the door. I stand and look through the peephole. I see two uniformed men standing there and my heart sinks into my stomach. I quickly unlock the door and open it.

"Ms. Rodrigues?" One of the men asks.

"Yes."

"I'm Major John Lanning and this is Major Michael Rand. We're here to inform you that Reinaldo

Vaz was involved in an enemy attack at the Embassy in Germany. We know he was injured but do not know the extent of his injuries," he says.

My hand comes up to my mouth and I start to shake my head. I feel my whole body starts trembling, and my legs are going to give out. Major Rand reaches out and grabs me before I fall. He picks me up and walks into the house. He sits me down in the chair I was sitting in. I bury my face in my hands and cry. This can't be happening. My whole world feels like it's crashing down on me. *Please, God, don't take him from me too. I need him so much.*

"Are you okay, ma'am?" he asks but I can't speak. I nod.

"Ms. Rodrigues, there's a plane ready to take you to the hospital he was taken to. As far as we know, he's alive," Major Lanning tells me.

I nod again but I can't find my voice. *I love him so much and I can't go through this again. I can't lose him. Oh God, I can't lose him.*

"Do you need to pack anything?" I shake my head.

"I'm already packed. I was supposed to leave tomorrow for Germany." I point to the two suitcases and a bag behind them. Major Rand picks them up and heads to the door.

"Well, that's convenient. Let's get going then. The plane's leaving in an hour."

I jump up and wipe my face. Somehow, I will myself to be strong. I quickly grab my laptop, purse, and cell phone. I lock the door behind me and place the keys in the lockbox on the door. I follow both of the Majors to the car and we're off.

Chapter 30

Kat

When I get to the base, I check into security and follow Major Lanning. They give my luggage to a soldier, who quickly places it on the plane.

Major Lanning turns to me. "This is as far as we go. I wish you a safe flight and we're praying Major Vaz is okay." He places his hand out and I take it. We shake hands.

"Thank you, sir." I look at Corporal Rand and he nods his head at me.

The soldier comes up and helps me step onto the stairs that lead to the plane. I quickly go up the stairs and step onto the plane. Another soldier helps me to a seat. I sit and fasten my seat belt. I place my purse on my lap, close my eyes, and say a quick prayer. I open my eyes and look around. There's nothing luxurious about this plane. *Was this plane used for this purpose only?* My heart sinks at that thought…that's terrible. Just then, another woman walks into the plane and the same soldier leads her to the seat across from me. She mirrors what I did and quickly fastens her seatbelt. Her cheeks are stained with tears and her eyes are bloodshot. She looks just like I do. I haven't stopped crying. She looks at me and gives me a small smile. I do the same.

The soldier walks up. "We'll be taking off in five minutes," he informs us and goes back to his post next to the plane entrance.

I close my eyes and pray. *Please God, watch over Rey. Please don't let him die. He's my whole world. I need him, and we need to see what our future holds.* Everything's happening so fast. My mind is whirling, and the same thoughts keep running in an endless loop through my mind.

I feel myself shaking and I can feel the tears falling from my eyes. Suddenly, the plane starts moving and I jerk. I keep my eyes tightly closed until the plane is in the air. After a few minutes, the soldier walks up to us again.

"You may remove your seatbelts and walk around if you need to."

"Thank you." The other woman and I say in unison.

The soldier walks away, and I look at the other woman. She looks to be about my age and my heart breaks for her. I know exactly how she feels, and I don't ever want anyone to feel like this. I unbuckle my seatbelt and walk up to her. She looks up at me and I extend my hand.

"My name is Kat." She takes my hand and shakes it.

"I'm Samantha."

"Nice to meet you, even if it is under these circumstances." She shakes her head and starts to cry. I sit in the seat next to her and take her into my arms. I hold her and let her cry. My tears fall as well. I don't know how much time has gone by. She's now able to compose herself.

"I'm so sorry." She pulls away and wipes the tears from her face.

"There's no need to apologize," I say. "I'm sorry for whatever you're going through."

"By the look on your face, we're going through the same thing." I nod. "My husband was involved in some incident at the American Embassy in Germany. They tell me he's injured but can't tell me how bad."

"Same here only he's not my husband. He's my boyfriend," I say, and she nods. "Do you have any children?"

"No. We're waiting until his term is up. He finishes in a month."

"I'm sure he'll be okay. Then, you can start with your beautiful family."

"From your mouth to God's ears," she whispers.

We talk for the rest of the flight. We speak about our relationships and the different life experiences we've had and our careers. We bond in a sense. It's nice to share my feelings with someone impartial to my life. We exchange email addresses and phone numbers. I know I just created an unbelievable friendship. We promise to email each other as soon as we know the conditions of our men. Having someone who understands what you're going through is worth more than anyone realizes.

****

When we land, we're taken to a hospital about an hour from the base. When we get to the hospital, each one of us has a soldier escort into the building. Each soldier gets the information they need from hospital personnel and turns to us.

"Ms. Rodrigues, I need to take you to the fourth floor." The soldier with the name Brown on his uniform says and I nod my understanding.

"Mrs. Lucas, I need to take you to the sixth floor." The soldier with the name of Smalls on his uniform says and she also nods.

I turn and look at Samantha. "Good luck. I hope he's okay. Keep your head up."

"Thank you. Same to you."

We give each other a quick hug and I turn to follow Officer Brown to the fourth floor. We go up in the elevators. When the doors open on the fourth floor, the sign says the Intensive Care Unit. My heart begins to pound hard, and my eyes become flooded with tears. *Oh God, please let him be okay.* I start to panic. We're buzzed in through the double doors and I'm taken to room three. As I walk through the door, I see Rey. He's lying there with his eyes closed, a breathing tube down his throat, and machines hooked up to almost every inch of his body. His right arm and leg are bandaged up. I bring my hand to my mouth and start to cry. I walk closer to him and look at him. His right cheek is bruised, and he has scratches all over.

I sink into the chair closest to the bed and just let go. I stay as quiet as possible, but I can't believe this is Rey. This can't be happening. I feel a hand on my shoulder, and I look up. A man is standing next to me wearing a white lab coat. He has short hair and a trimmed beard. He has light brown eyes that show so much kindness. He doesn't look like a local. He gives me a small smile and a nod. I wipe my face and stand.

"Hello, I'm Dr. Barns. I've been treating Major Vaz since he was brought in," he says.

"I'm Katarina Rodrigues. I'm his girlfriend." It's all I can manage to say.

"Let me check his chart and we'll talk." He walks to the foot of Rey's bed. He picks up the chart and reads through a few pages. He walks around to Rey's right side. He checks the bandages and does a check of his eyes. He places his little flashlight in his pocket and turns to me.

"How's he doing?" I'm looking at the doctor with pleading eyes and hoping he gives me the good news.

"Well, we have him in here because his injuries are serious. He's been unconscious since he was brought in. His CT scan showed he has a concussion but there was no swelling. I don't believe there's any injury to the brain, but we'll know for sure once he wakes up. He lost a lot of blood from his arm and leg, and we had to give him a transfusion. His arm and his leg have severe lacerations, which I have stitched up. The one on the leg severed a small section of the artery, but I was able to repair it. There's no significant muscle damage I can see. He will need physical therapy, but I don't expect any complications." He tells me.

"Why does he have a breathing tube in?" I ask through tears.

"He wasn't breathing well when he was brought in. It was his body's reaction to the pain and trauma, so I put the breathing tube in to help him. He has no lung damage or broken ribs. We'll remove it as soon as he wakes up." He smiles at me reassuringly.

"So, he's going to be okay?" I ask, sobbing and looking at Rey.

"I expect him to make a full recovery. Once he wakes up, almost all these machines will come off him and he'll be moved to a regular room." I start to cry harder when I hear those words. *Thank you, God, for not taking him away from me.*

"Is there anything I can do to help him wake up?"

"Talk to him. It's all you can do." I extend my hand.

"Thank you so much, Doctor. Thank you for taking such good care of him," I say.

He takes my hand and shakes it. "You're very welcome, Ms. Rodrigues." He turns to walk away. When he gets to the doorway, he turns. "I'll be checking on him periodically."

"Thank you." I turn toward Rey and get up from the chair. I walk up to his bedside. I put my hand on his and lean down so I'm near his ear.

"I'm here, baby. Please wake up. I need you to wake up. After so long, I'm finally next to you but you're lying in a hospital bed. This isn't what I expected when I finally got to you." I wipe the tears away. I compose myself and lean toward his ear again. "I love you. You're my world. I need you to wake up, sweetheart." I kiss his cheek and turn to pull the chair next to the bed. I sit there, watching him, and praying.

Chapter 31

Kat

I've been sitting in this chair for two hours and Rey hasn't moved an inch. I get up and pace the room. This waiting is going to drive me insane. What will happen if he doesn't wake up? All kinds of worst-case scenarios keep popping into my head. I shake my head. Rey's nurse comes in to check his vitals again. I smile when she walks in.

"Have you had anything to eat?" she asks with a very thick accent.

"No. I'm not hungry," I respond.

"Would you like some coffee?" She walks up to me and smiles.

"I could do that."

"Follow me." I follow her to a small room. The only things in the room are a coffee machine and a small refrigerator. She pours me a cup of coffee and hands it to me. "There's sugar right there and milk in the icebox."

"Thank you so much. I'm sorry, I didn't catch your name," I say.

"My name is Anna."

"I'm Kat. Thank you for taking such good care of Rey."

"You're most welcome. Feel free to get coffee anytime you would like. If there's anything you need, please let me know." She walks back to her station.

I add milk and sugar to my coffee and walk back into Rey's room. I sit in the chair again and sip my coffee. I look at Rey and my mind goes back to John's wedding. We had such a good time. We danced and laughed; it was the night we first time made love. It was a magical night. I think about the way he smiled at me and how he looked at me. My heart swells. I stand again and go to his bedside. I place my hand on his again and just stand there for a little while.

****

Another two hours have gone by. I'm pacing Rey's room again. I only walk away from him to go to the bathroom or to get coffee. He still hasn't moved an inch and I'm starting to worry he won't wake up. Just then, Dr. Barns walks into the room.

"Hello, Ms. Rodrigues."

"Hi, Doctor. Please call me Kat." He nods.

"Okay, Kat. How's the patient?" he says as he looks at Rey.

"No change. I'm starting to worry he isn't waking up," I tell him.

"Let me check his chart and do a quick exam and we'll talk." I step out of his way and let him do his job.

He picks up the chart and reads it again. Once he's done, he puts on gloves. He walks up to Rey's bandaged arm and proceeds to remove the bandage. He checks the wound and rewraps it. He removes the bandage from his leg. He does some maneuvers on his leg. I see the wound on his leg and feel my stomach turn. It looks so nasty. It has to be painful. Anna walks in with a tube of something in her hand. She smiles at me and walks up to the Doctor. She takes the cap off it and hands it to the Doctor. He applies it to the wound. They put a new bandage on his leg and Dr. Barns removes the gloves. He throws them in the garbage and walks to the sink. He washes and dries his hands. He takes the little flashlight out of his pocket and walks back to Rey. He examines his eyes again and turns to me.

"His vitals are really good and strong. His wounds are clean and healing nicely. His eyes are clear. I can't give you a reason as to why he hasn't woken up yet. If he hasn't woken up by tomorrow morning, I'm going to order another CT scan just to be sure. I know it's difficult, but it's a waiting game at this point," he says.

"Thank you."

"I'll be at the nurse's station for another hour. After, I'll be leaving for the evening," he tells me.

"Okay." He walks out. I walk back up to Rey, lean down, and kiss his cheek. I run my hand through his hair. "Wake up, baby. You need to wake up." I run my hand through his hair one more time and sit down.

I place my hand on his and watch his face. I look down at his hand and see his fingers move. I jump up. I watch his face and see he's trying to open his eyes. I go to the door quickly. Dr. Barns looks up as I get to the doorway.

"I think he's waking up." He stands, and I go back to Rey. When I get back to him, his eyes open. He stares at the ceiling. Dr. Barns comes in and goes to the other side of the bed.

"Major Vaz," Dr. Barns says. Rey turns his head toward the doctor. Dr. Barns checks his eyes with his flashlight again. He smiles and tells him not to talk. Rey looks back up at the ceiling and Dr. Barns leaves the room.

I lean in toward him. "Thank you for waking up, my love." He turns his head and looks at me. I feel the tears falling from my eyes as he stares at me. Dr. Barns walks back into the room with Nurse Anna following him.

"Kat, we need to remove his breathing tube," Dr. Barns says.

I move away from Rey's bed and let the nurse and doctor do what they need to do. I stand by the door and thank God for letting him be okay. I bury my face in my hands and breathe a sigh of relief. I've shed too many tears and I'm over it. I look up and see the tube and other machines are removed from him. Dr. Barns waves me over and Anna leaves the room.

I walk over to Rey. He's watching me walk toward him. I place my hand on his and smile. For a second, I worry he doesn't recognize me. That can't be the case. But the look in his eyes tells me he knows very well who I am.

"Hi, baby."

"Hi," he says with a very raspy voice. He coughs and the doctor pats his shoulder.

"Anna's coming back with ice chips. Your throat will feel better within the next couple of hours," Dr. Barns tells him. Rey doesn't take his eyes off me. "I'm Dr. Barns. I've been treating you since you were brought in." He continues to tell him about his condition and that he'll be moving to another room. Anna walks back in and hands me the ice chips. I scoop some onto the spoon and bring it up to his lips. He opens his mouth and I feed him. He hasn't looked away from me.

"Major Vaz, I need you to look at me and acknowledge your understanding of what I said," Dr. Barns says.

Rey turns his head toward Dr. Barns. "Sorry." He coughs.

"Do you understand what I explained to you?"

"Yes, sir."

"Good. I'll arrange for your room transfer and will be leaving for the evening," he says. "I'll check on you first thing tomorrow morning." He taps Rey's shoulder and walks around to me. He shakes my hand.

"Thank you."

He walks out of the room, and I turn to Rey. He's watching me again. I give him some more ice chips and smile at him.

"I love you." He gives me a weak smile.

"I love you," he whispers. "It's so nice to see your face. I've missed you."

Chapter 32

Rey

I wake up and immediately see Kat sleeping on the couch by the window. I was moved out of ICU and into a private room in the middle of the night. Kat and the nurses make sure I have everything I need. I'm so happy to see Kat is finally getting some rest, even if it's only a few hours. I watch her sleep. She's beautiful. She's lying on her side and her head rests on her hand. This is not how I imagined us reuniting. Damn it. I planned on picking her up at the airport, taking her to our new apartment, and making love to her all night. I guess it will have to wait a while now.

I look down at my arm and leg. They hurt so damn bad. Therapy's going to kill me, but I'm ready to start moving. Laying here and watching everyone do everything for me sucks. I need to move around. I move a little and groan. The pain that shoots up my leg is enough to make me stop breathing.

The nurse walks in and smiles. I place my finger to my lips and point to Kat. She nods her head. She checks my IV and vitals.

"How's the pain?" she asks.

"It doesn't hurt too much until I move."

"In an hour, we'll be taking you for a CT scan and the therapist will be in later to work with you. I'm sure you're dying to move around."

I nod. "Yes, I am."

"In between the CT scan and the therapist, the doctor will be in to see you," she continues. "If you need anything, please don't hesitate to ask."

"Thank you, ma'am."

"Why is he going for another CT scan?" Kat asks, and both the nurse and I look at her. *When did she wake up?*

"The doctor just wants to be cautious." She smiles at Kat.

"Okay, thank you," Kat says as she stands. The nurse washes her hands and walks out of the room. Kat walks over to me.

"How are you feeling this morning?" she asks me as she leans down to kiss my cheek.

"I'm okay. My throat isn't sore anymore, but my arm and leg kill when I move around. I'm dying to stand up and move, regardless of the pain," I tell her.

"I know but you can't yet. You will this afternoon," she reassures. "Are you thirsty?"

"A little."

"I'll get you some water." She's about to step away when I grab her hand. She looks down at my hand and into my eyes.

"I'm sorry this is what you have to deal with when we're finally reunited. This isn't what I imagined for us."

"I know. I'm just grateful you're alive. You scared the crap out of me." Tears swell in her eyes. I close my eyes. I hate seeing the tears. I hate it more knowing it was me that put those tears in her eyes.

"I'm so sorry, baby. The bomb came out of nowhere and we couldn't seek cover. It all happened so fast."

"I keep thanking God you're alive. I hope whoever did this to you and the others paid for what they did. Now, we need to focus on getting you one hundred percent so we can move on with our lives." She leans down and kisses my lips gently. She pulls away and looks at me. "Thank you for coming back to me. I thought I was going to lose my mind waiting to see those beautiful eyes."

I swallow hard. She smiles, kisses my hand, and picks up the empty pitcher. She walks out of the room. A minute later, she's back. She pours me a cup of water, puts a straw in it, and walks over to me. She places the straw in my mouth, and I drink. I watch her face as I drink. She has black rings under her eyes and looks so tired. She notices me watching her and smiles at me.

"Want some more?" she asks as I finish with the water.

"No, I'm okay for now. Thank you."

"No problem. Let me know when you want more." I can tell by the way she walks around the room that she's extremely stressed. I feel terrible because I know I'm doing this to her. This is the last thing I ever wanted to do to her. I'm seriously rethinking if I want to re-up after my contract is up. I have two more years under this contract if they don't discharge me, which I believe is coming. I have a lot of thinking to do, and I'll have to talk to Kat. I need to know how she feels about it. I know she can endure anything. She's so strong, and I know she'll tell me to follow my heart and do what makes me happy. Either way, we need to have the conversation and soon.

Chapter 33

Kat

Rey's been taken for a CT scan and I'm sitting on the couch waiting for him. I hate hospitals and I can't wait to get the hell out of here. Too many bad memories keep creeping up on me. Rey seems to be okay physically although he still has a long road ahead of him. Therapy is going to be rough, but his leg and arm will return to normal. I sit and silently thank God Rey will be fine. I know something isn't right with him though. He seems so distant. It seems as if he has something weighing on his mind. I'm pretty sure he's worried about his contract and how his injury will impact it. I don't want to pressure him into telling me what he's thinking about, but I need to make sure he knows we'll be fine. He needs to understand our life will be fine, military or not. I love him more than life itself and nothing will get in the way of that. We can make anything work as long as we are together.

I stand and start pacing the room. I feel like I'm wasting time just sitting here. I know I can't do anything for Rey but I'm still restless and anxious. I need to do something. I go back to the couch and pick up my bag. I pull out my laptop and open my email. I shoot a quick email to my editor. I let her know I have three new book ideas and want them all to be published by the end of the year. I also tell her I'm ready to do book signings. I ask her to set up a preliminary signing schedule and to shoot me an email. I thank her for her help and close my laptop.

Just then, Rey is being rolled back into the room. He's sitting up in bed. I stand and watch as the tech locks his bed into place and walks out. I go to him and place my hand on his shoulder. He smiles at me.

"How are you feeling?" I ask as I run my hand through his hair. He closes his eyes at the contact.

"Sore but okay," he says and moans. "That feels good."

I continue to stroke his hair and he seems to relax a bit. I continue doing it for another five minutes when the doctor walks in. He walks up to Rey's side.

"Good morning," Dr. Barns says.

Rey opens his eyes and looks at the doctor.

"Good morning."

"Good morning, Dr. Barns," I say with a smile.

"How are you feeling this morning, Major?" Dr. Barns asks Rey.

"I'm sore, but fine for the most part."

"That's good to hear. Your CT scan was normal. Your bruises and small lacerations are healing nicely."

"Great," Rey says, and I watch his face. Something's bothering him, but he isn't asking the questions he has floating around in his mind.

"I'm going to check your arm and leg and we'll talk further about those two injuries," Dr. Barns says and Rey nods. The doctor steps out and calls for the nurse as he puts on the gloves. He walks over to Rey and starts to remove the bandages from Rey's leg and arm. The nurse comes in and starts shuffling through the cabinets getting antiseptic, ointments, gauze, and tape. She brings all of it over to the small table next to the doctor. She walks back to the sink and washes her hands and puts on a pair of gloves. The doctor is examining the wounds. He's pressing on the edges of the wound. The nurse lifts Rey's leg and the doctor asks Rey to bend his knee.

I watch Rey's face as he bends his knee. He doesn't look like he's pushing himself or asserting too much effort on bending his knee. I'm certain it's a good sign. The doctor maneuvers Rey's leg to the left and the right and Rey doesn't flinch. The doctor puts his leg down and the nurse hands him some gauze with antiseptic and goes to work getting the ointment ready. The doctor wipes at the wound and throws the gauze in the garbage. He takes the ointment from the nurse and applies it to the wound liberally. Dr. Barns and the nurse work together to wrap the wound back up.

Dr. Barns walks over to the sink, removes his gloves, and washes his hands again. He grabs a fresh pair of gloves and walks back to Rey. He checks the wound on his arm and asks Rey to bend his arm and wiggle his fingers. Rey does it effortlessly. The doctor and the nurse repeat the process of wound care and bandaging the wound. The doctor walks back to the sink and removes his gloves. He washes his hands yet again and pulls out his pen. He writes his notes on the chart as the nurse bustles around the room cleaning up. I stroke Rey's hair as we wait. He looks up at me. I can see the worry in his eyes. I lean down and whisper in his ear.

"Everything will be fine." I pull away from his ear and smile a reassuring smile at him. He nods as I place my other hand up on top of his good hand. He laces his fingers through mine and squeezes. The doctor walks up and smiles at Rey.

"I'm very pleased with the way your injuries are healing. The wounds are very clean with no signs of infection. You seemed to have bent your knee and arm nicely with no signs of pain or discomfort. I had to repair a small tear in the artery that runs through your leg, but there don't seem to be any complications from that," he says. "Therapy will be starting this afternoon. I don't expect any complications with therapy, and you'll be good as new within the next four to six weeks. I want to keep you here another day and then you can go home."

Rey smiles at him and I see him release the breath he was holding.

"Thank you, Doctor," Rey says. "Will I continue to see you once I'm discharged from the hospital?"

"Yes. My office information will be in your discharge papers. I want to see you every week until you're discharged from therapy. Therapy will be at a rehab center I work within the same building where my office is located. You'll have therapy there twice a week. How does that sound?"

"It sounds perfect. Thank you so much for everything."

"Do you have any other questions?"

"No, sir." Dr. Barns nods.

"Now, I have a question for Ms. Kat," Dr. Barns says, and I look at him. I can feel Rey turn to look at me.

"Yes, Doctor."

"When was the last time you ate?" I can feel my face get hot.

"Um...I had lunch before I was told about what happened to Rey. I haven't had anything since then." I look at Rey. He closes his eyes.

"So, you haven't had anything to eat in two days?" Dr. Barns asks.

"About that."

"You need to go get something to eat immediately. You can't do this, Ms. Kat. You'll end up next to Major here if you don't take care of yourself. I can see you're an extremely strong woman, but you need to give your body fuel, or you will run yourself down and you won't be any good to anyone."

"I know. I promise to get something to eat."

"I'm sorry, Ms. Kat. I just don't want to see you sick. You've been extremely nice to every member of this staff since you've been here. We rarely get someone like you here and we don't want to see you as a patient." Dr. Barns smiles and looks at Rey. "You're a very lucky man. She hasn't left your side and I can see she'll do anything for you."

"I know, sir. I know how lucky I am." Rey looks at me. "I'll make sure she gets something to eat right away."

"Good. Rest up and I'll see you tomorrow morning. If you need me before then, just let the nurses know." He extends his hand to Rey.

"Thank you. I appreciate it." Rey shakes his hand with his injured one. The doctor smiles. He looks at me and nods his head.

"Thank you," I say as he walks out.

Chapter 34

Kat

Rey looks at me and I can see the worry written all over his face. He presses the nurse button without taking his eyes away from mine. A few seconds later, the nurse walks in.

"Yes, Major Vaz."

"Where can Kat go get some food?" She looks at me and smiles.

"On the first floor, you'll find three restaurants. One makes hot meals; another is a sandwich shop and the other is a coffee shop."

"Thank you." Both of us say at once. She laughs and leaves the room.

"Go downstairs and get something to eat right now." I put both my hands up in surrender.

"I'm going." I lean down and kiss his lips. His hand comes up and cups the back of my head. I pull back a little and he pushes me back down to his mouth. He kisses me passionately. When our kiss breaks, I lean my forehead on his. "I've missed you so much."

"I've missed you too, baby, so much. Nothing will take me away from you," he says. "Now go get some food."

I laugh and turn to grab my purse. I walk to the door and turn to him. He's watching me. I blow him a kiss and walk out.

****

Two hours later, I'm sitting on the couch working on an outline for a new book. Rey's napping. The nurse came in with his antibiotic and a few minutes after he took it, he fell asleep. I feel a bit better after I ate an egg and cheese sandwich and drank some orange juice. I was starting to feel weak. I knew I had to get food in me soon even though I wasn't hungry. Rey seems considerably better after the doctor left. I know he's worried about how permanent his injuries are and how his life's going to change. The doctor's prognosis is very good, and it calmed his fears. The visit with the therapist this afternoon will calm the rest of his fears. He'll see his injuries will require some work to overcome but he'll return to normal very quickly.

My email dings and I switch applications to check it. It's a message from my editor. She states she's thrilled I want to release three new books by the end of the year and even more excited I agreed to do signings. She explains many fans are constantly asking about meeting me. She gives me a list of all the signings she wants me to do. The list consists of about ten different signing conferences, plus a guest speaker at some of those conferences. She asks me to look through them and to let her know which ones I'm interested in. I email her back and tell her I'll look through all the material and get back to her as soon as possible.

I quickly skim the synopsis of the signings and the locations. There's a signing in England, Australia, New York, California, Texas, and Florida. I feel the excitement build and I smile. This will be fun, and a change of pace will be welcomed. I continue to read and hear Rey stir. I look up and see him looking at me. I place my laptop on the couch and stand. I walk over to him and kiss his forehead.

"How was your nap?" I ask.

"Great. I guess I needed it."

"Rey, what's bothering you?" I finally ask. "I wasn't going to ask, and I don't want to push, but I'm worried about what's going on in that brain of yours."

He laughs and looks up at me. I pull up the chair that's behind me and sit down.

"I've been worried my injuries won't allow me to return to service. It's not that I won't be able to continue my duties. I'm worried about what I'm going to do if I can't continue with the military." He says and sighs. I nod, and he continues. "I have a degree in criminal justice with a master's in forensic investigation. I've had some police training and do that now. I've never worked outside the military, and I don't know where I would start to try to do that. I don't know if they're going to wait or discharge me. I'm waiting to hear from my commanders."

"If given the chance, do you want to stay in the military?" I ask.

"I don't know. I panic when I think of not being in the military."

"With your degree and training, you can get a job working for any police department. I'm not worried about you getting a job. I'm worried about your happiness. Will you be happy not serving in the military? Will you be happy doing just forensic work? You're an intelligent man and will succeed wherever you go. I'll support any decision you make and I'm here to listen if you need me to. Unfortunately, this is a decision only you can make. I'll be happy with whatever you decide, as long as you're happy. It'll help in the decision process if you need me to answer questions, but the ultimate decision is strictly up to you."

He nods and looks down at his hands. "I'm afraid of making the wrong decision. I don't want to disappoint you or make you unhappy. I want to take care of you."

I place my hands on either side of his face and make him look at me.

"If you make a decision that doesn't work then we'll work together to get you to a place that does make you happy. You don't know unless you try. I'm happy as long as I'm with you. Jobs are easy to change. You can't be replaced, jobs can be," I say as a tear falls from his eye. I wipe it away and smile. "I'm not going anywhere, and we can get through anything together. Do what your heart tells you to do, and everything will fall into place." I kiss the tip of his nose and he laughs.

"Thank you. I'm a lucky man."

"Yes, you are," I agree, and we both laugh.

Chapter 35

Kat

The next morning, I wake and look at Rey. He's still sleeping, and I take a moment to watch him sleep. I sit up and stretch. I can't wait to get out of this hospital so I can take a shower and sleep in a real bed again. I'm exhausted, and my back's killing me. I pick up my cell phone and check the time. It's seven in the morning. I stand and head to the bathroom.

I walk out of the bathroom a few minutes later to find the nurse taking Rey's vitals. I smile at her and go back to the couch. The therapist's visit yesterday went very well. Rey walked a while, and he said the pain was minimal. The therapist was impressed with his movement and expects him to make a full recovery quickly. He believes he'll be back to normal in less than a month. He makes sure to stress that Rey will have to continue to exercise daily to keep his leg and arm healthy.

Rey's happy with what the therapist said. Throughout the afternoon, he would get up and take walks around the room and go to the bathroom on his own. That made him happy. He mentioned he was surprised he hadn't heard from his commanders yet. I told him I was sure they knew of his condition and that they wanted to let him rest.

The nurse finishes and waves on her way out. I watch him sleep. About five minutes later, there's a knock on the door and a uniformed man walks in. I stand and walk toward him. He extends his hand and I shake it.

"Hello. My name is Colonel Mike Martinez," he says, and I nod.

"It's nice to meet you, sir. My name is Kat."

"Nice to meet you, too. How's he doing?" he asks as he looks at Rey.

"He's doing well. We're expecting him to go home today."

"Good to hear." He walks up to Rey. "I need to speak to him. Would you mind waking him?" I place my hand on Rey's.

"Rey." I give his hand a small squeeze. He opens his eyes and looks at me. "Sorry to wake you but there's someone here who needs to speak to you." His eyes move and lock with his commander's. He quickly salutes him and brings the bed up to a sitting position.

"Major, how are you feeling?" Colonel Martinez asks.

"Much better, sir."

"Ms. Kat, would you mind leaving us to talk in private for a few minutes?"

"Of course." I look at Rey. "I'm going to get breakfast and return some emails." He nods. I pick up my laptop, and purse, and quickly leave the room.

****

An hour later, I close my laptop and grab my purse. I clean off my table and head for the elevator. I press the button and wait for the elevator to arrive. Once it arrives, the doors open, and I see Colonel Martinez. He nods at me.

"Good day," he says.

"You, too," I respond and watch him exit the hospital.

I get into the elevator and head back to Rey's room. When I reach his room, I lightly knock.

"Come in." I hear Rey say. I step in and close the door behind me. "You don't have to knock."

"I just wanted to be sure it was safe to come in. I saw your commander leave the hospital, but I just wanted to be sure." He holds out his hand for me. "Are you okay?"

"Yeah." He leans his head back. "He came to give me my choices."

"Choices?"

"I have the choice to be honorably discharged or retire," he tells me.

"Oh, Rey. I'm so sorry." I look down at my feet. I have no idea what to say to him.

"I'm not."

"I'm confused." I sit in the chair next to the bed. He opens his eyes and looks at me. He looks happy and content. After the talk yesterday, I was sure he would be very stressed by what his commander had to say.

"I knew this was coming. This type of injury is career-ending in the service. Not because of the physical injury but the mental injury. Once a soldier endures this type of injury, the military feels you won't be able to do their job properly for fear of getting hurt again. They can't afford an unfocused soldier." He takes a deep breath and continues. "I was terrified about what I'd do when this happened. I was so scared I would lose you. So, I was wracking my brain trying to figure out what I would do when this came about until you forced me to tell you what I was worried about yesterday. You made me see the military is a career and not my whole life. I've learned a lot and I'll always have a love for the military, but I'm excited for the next chapter in my life. I want freedom. I want the freedom to live where we want and to do what I want to do." He smiles at me, and I can't help but smile back. "I realize I can do what I always wanted to do, and I can do it from wherever I want."

"What do you want to do?" I ask, watching the joy play across his face.

"I want to teach. I've always wanted to be a teacher. I decided to forget about it once I joined the military, but you reminded me of my passion. I want to teach forensics," he says.

"That's amazing! I'm so happy you get to do what you've always wanted to do!" I jump off the chair. I wrap my arms around him and hug him tightly. He hugs me just as tightly. I feel the familiar jolt in my belly whenever he's around. His touch is like electricity running through my body and I want him so badly. I pull away from him and kiss him softly. "I'm so proud of the man you are. You're brave and selfless, and you have a heart of gold."

"Thank you, baby, for everything."

"You don't need to thank me, but I need to thank you. You saved me. I don't know what would've happened to me if I continued on the path I was on. You took me out of that funk, and I can never repay you."

"Let's call it even," he says as we laugh.

Chapter 36

Rey

Two weeks later, I'm going full speed on the elliptical machine in therapy. I'm walking without a cane to help me, and I barely have a limp. I have full control of my arm and a very small amount of pain. I'm feeling great, all things considered. Kat and I are great except we haven't been able to make love due to my injury. The doctor has given me strict restrictions and I have to be released by the therapist to return to certain activities. It's killing me not to be able to show her how much I love her.

I decided to retire from the military. Kat supports me one hundred percent. Because the injury forced me to retire, they gave me a lump sum and I get to keep my military benefits and pension. It's a sweet deal and I'm glad to be starting this new chapter in my life. Kat, by far, has been the most rewarding. She's amazing and takes such good care of me. We still have a month left on our lease and we don't know where we want to go yet. We're only taking clothes and buying everything new in our new home. We're both so excited but can't decide where to go. We love Europe, but we also don't want to be so far away from my parents, especially since they're getting older.

My therapist, Stephen, walks up and takes me out of my trance.

"You're doing great, Rey. Let's do your stretching." He stops the machine. I step off and follow him to a table. I lie down, and Stephen starts to stretch and massage my arm. "How does it feel? Any pain?"

"No, I'm feeling great."

"Good. Let me know if you feel any pain." He continues stretching and massaging my arm. After a few minutes, he moves to my leg. After a few minutes of that, my arm and leg are covered in ice. "Still no pain?"

"Nope." I smile at him. He writes some notes on my chart and looks up at me.

"One more week of therapy and you'll be discharged," Stephen says with a wide grin on his face.

"That's great!" I extend my hand and he shakes it.

"You did great work, Rey. I want you to continue to do regular workouts, but I don't see why you need more than one more week. You're using both your arm and leg fully." He stands.

"Thanks, Stephen. I appreciate your help. Now, I have a question."

"Shoot."

"Can I please be cleared to make love to my girl?" Stephen starts laughing. "Why are you laughing man? I'm serious."

"I know you're serious. That's why it's funny." Stephen shakes his head and picks up my chart again. He starts writing. "Mr. Vaz is cleared to return to all activities. No restrictions." He looks up at me and gives me a big smile. "You may go make love to your girl."

"Thanks, man!" I give him a big smile back. He removes the ice from my arm and leg, and I get up.

I shake Stephen's hand one more time and head home.

****

I walk into our apartment and place my keys down in the bowl sitting on the foyer table. I go into the kitchen, but she isn't there. As I head to our bedroom, I hear the shower running and I smile. I go into the bathroom and strip as quickly and as quietly as I can. Once undressed, I move the curtain and look in. Her back is to me, and she has her face under the water stream. I step in and place my arms around her. She jumps a little and turns her face to me. She smiles.

"Hi, baby," she purrs.

"Hi." I kiss her. She turns in my arms, and I deepen the kiss. When we break apart, I move my head to kiss her neck. "I want you so bad."

"I want you to, but you haven't gotten the clearance yet. I don't want you to get hurt again." She gives me a small moan and I nearly lose it. I move back a little and look into her beautiful eyes.

"I was cleared to resume all activities," I tell her, and she smiles. "Plus, one more week of therapy and I'll be discharged."

"That's great!" Her arms come around my neck. "I'm so proud of you."

I kiss her again and she kisses me back with the same need I have for her. I deepen the kiss and we kiss as if we're trying to breathe in air from each other's lungs. I push her up against the shower wall. She immediately brings her legs up and wraps them around my waist.

"Oh God, I missed you so much." I kiss down her neck to her chest and her breasts. She leans her head back and closes her eyes. She lets out a small moan again.

"I've missed you, too." She barely gets out. Her hands are in my hair and she's pushing my head closer to her. I move back up to her lips and kiss her hard. "I need you now."

I look at her and she looks at my mouth and back into my eyes. I position myself and enter her slowly. Her hands run along my shoulders, my back, and my ass. She grabs my ass and pushes me deeper into her. I bury myself in her and moan. Nothing feels better than this.

"You feel amazing." I start to move. I can feel her tightening around me, and I know she's already shattering. She calls out my name and holds onto me so tightly. When her breathing slows, I start moving again but this time I know I won't be able to stop. She's so tight and warm and it's taking everything out of me not to release. I start thrusting hard into her and we both come together, calling out each other's names. We stay like this until we can both breathe normally again.

"I love you, sweetheart," I whisper in her ear.

"I love you," she says with a wide grin.

I let her down and we bathe each other. Once we're both clean and toweled up, I pick her up and carry her to our bed. I make love to her two more times before we continue with our day.

Chapter 37

Kat

Making love with Rey is always mind-blowing. It's a complete out-of-body experience every single time. I love every moment we spend together. He's so gentle yet so passionate. He gives himself completely to me. I give myself completely to him right back, mind and soul. He makes me feel beautiful and sexy. He makes sure I feel loved, and I can only hope I'm doing the same for him.

Rey and I are sitting at the dining room table. Both of us have our laptops open in front of us. He's researching teaching positions and I'm working on another outline. I have one done and two more to go. He looks up from his laptop.

"Have you given any more thought to where you want to live?" he asks.

"Yes, but I can't decide." I cross my hands in front of my face and lay my chin on them. "Your parents are in North Carolina. Don't you want to be close to them?"

"Yes, but it doesn't mean we have to live in the same state. I want to be somewhere where I can get to them fairly quickly if they need me. Being on another continent isn't convenient," he says. "I'm sorry. I feel like I'm forcing you to be someplace you don't want to be."

I push my chair back and stand. I walk around the table and sit on his lap. I gather his face in my hands. "You're not forcing me to do anything. Being next to family is important, especially since they're getting older. I get it. I'm excited about being close to your parents. It's been a long time since I spent some time with family."

"You have no idea how much I love that you think of my parents as your family." He kisses me.

"I say we move to North Carolina. If your parents are okay with it, we can stay with them until we find a house."

"I love that idea. I wanted to mention it before but didn't want to shove my parents down your throat."

"Please tell me what you're thinking always and trust me to tell you if I disagree with it," I say.

"I promise. I'll call my parents and see what they think about it. Let's call them together tonight." I smile at him and kiss his nose. I stand and go back to work.

****

A few hours later, Rey's talking to his mother on the phone. He asks her to put the phone on speaker and his dad comes on the line. I walk up next to him.

"We're both here," Luisa says.

"Hi, Luisa and Paul," I greet.

"Hello, dear."

"Hello, Kat," Paul says.

"How are you both?"

"We're doing well. How are you?" Luisa tells me.

"I'm doing well."

"Hi, Dad," Rey says.

"Hi, son. How are you?"

"I'm well. I wanted you both on the line because Kat and I want to share some news with you and ask a favor."

"Well, let's hear it," Luisa says. Rey looks at me and smiles.

"Kat and I are moving to North Carolina," he blurts.

"Oh, that's wonderful!" Luisa exclaims. "I'm so happy to hear that!"

"That's great!" Paul says. "When will the move happen?"

"In two weeks," Rey tells them.

"Wonderful! So, what's the favor?" Paul asks.

"Can we stay with you until we find a house?"

"Absolutely!" Luisa responds quickly. "Stay as long as you want. It'll be nice to have you both here."

"I agree," Paul says.

"Thank you so much. We appreciate it and promise not to overstay our welcome," I tell them.

"Sweetheart, you could never overstay your welcome. We love you both and can't wait to see you," Paul says.

"Thanks, Mom and Dad."

"You're welcome," they say in unison.

"I'll call you and give you the details next week." A minute later, we say our goodbyes and hang up.

"That went well," Rey says with a wide smile on his beautiful face.

"It sure did. They seemed happy with the decision." A thought pops into my head. *Has Rey told them they won't ever be grandparents? Were they excited about us moving close by because they expect grandchildren?* I stand and walk into the kitchen. Rey follows me.

"What's wrong?" he asks, as I lean into the fridge and grab a Diet Coke. I pop the top of the soda. I take a long sip of my soda and look up at him.

"Have you told your parents I can't have children?"

"No. I haven't spoken to my parents about any part of our relationship." He takes a beer out of the fridge and opens it. He takes a long swig.

"You need to tell them. I know the main reason they're so excited is that they think they'll be close to their grandchildren." I close my eyes. "Oh God, they're going to be so disappointed and probably hate me."

"Baby, they may be disappointed, but they won't hate you. Their disappointment won't have anything to do with you. They love you and know what you've gone through. Mom and Dad told me how much they feel for you and what you endured. They'll be fine. I promise you." He comes closer to me. His arms come around me and he brings me in for a hug. I rest my head on his chest and can hear his heartbeat. "They could never hate you. They love you too much."

"I feel like I'm letting you and your family down." Tears fall down my face.

Rey places a finger under my chin and lifts my face. I look into his eyes. I don't see any sadness. He's truly happy.

"You're not letting me or anyone else down. Things happen. It is what it is, and life goes on. You can't control what happened. I love you and I'm so grateful to have you in my life. Children would have been a plus, but I'm not upset about the situation. I love you more than anything and I just want you," he says as he strokes my hair.

"I should be the one to tell them and to apologize to them," I say.

"You have nothing to apologize for and I can tell them. You don't need to relive it. I know how much it kills you to tell the story."

"I appreciate it, but I need to tell them." I wipe my face. "I'm so scared they'll hate me."

"They won't. They will understand." He leans down and kisses me. "I promise you."

Chapter 38

Kat

A week later, we land at Asheville Regional Airport in North Carolina. It's been a long trip with a very long layover at LaGuardia Airport in New York. Rey's kept me sane through the trip. I didn't get any sleep. I don't sleep on planes. I caught up on some reading though. When I wasn't reading, I was watching Rey sleep or talking to him. We talked about our plans for our new house and our timeline. We hope we can find the house we want quickly.

We meet Rey's parents at the baggage claim. Hugs are exchanged and the bell rings, indicating the carousel is about to start moving. Rey and Paul gather our bags and we head out. When we get outside, I take a deep breath of fresh air. The air is so clean here, even at the airport. I follow Rey and his parents to their car. Rey and I climb into the backseat of their SUV and we're off.

The drive to Paul and Luisa's house is breathtaking. The mountain views are spectacular. I did a little research about Asheville before we came. I know this part of North Carolina has the highest mountain peaks in the eastern United States. The western side mountains are best known for whitewater rafting, mountain biking, and hiking. The mountains have rollercoaster-like bike trails and natural waterslides. I can't wait to go hiking.

I look at Rey and notice he's watching me. I smile at him as he reaches out for my hand and kisses my palm.

"It's so beautiful here," I tell him.

"It is. I can't wait to take you hiking. You're going to love it." I laugh. "What's so funny?"

"I was just thinking about how I can't wait to go hiking."

"Great minds."

Rey proceeds to tell his parents our timeline. Paul informs Rey that he's contacted their real estate friend and she's willing to meet with us tomorrow and the rest of the week as we need her. She needs us to call her with what we're looking for, so she can set things up. Paul hands Rey his cell phone and tells him to call her so she has enough time to do her research. Rey dials her number and tells her what we're looking for. When he hangs up, he looks at me.

"We're meeting with her at ten o'clock tomorrow. She says a new property came on the market today that fits our criteria. She wants us to see that property first and go from there."

"Sounds great," I say as Paul pulls into their driveway.

I look up at the house. It's gorgeous. It's a two-story, all-stone house. Paul's a landscaper, so the landscaping is immaculate. The house is painted white with a red front door. The driveway and walkway up to the front door are all in stone. The house has a two-car garage. Luisa's car sits in the garage. Paul parks the SUV just outside the garage and we all get out. We get the luggage out of the trunk and head inside.

The inside of the house is even more beautiful. It's an open plan. The kitchen, family room, and dining room are all open. From every angle, you can see every part of this area. The kitchen has a light wood color, and the granite countertops are dark with stainless steel appliances. The furniture all over the house is very modern.

"Mom, the kitchen looks great!" Rey says.

"Thank you, honey. I'm just glad it's over. Renovations are a pain in the ass." She laughs.

"Luisa, your house is beautiful," I say, as Rey and Paul head up the stairs with our luggage.

"Thank you. Come on. I'll show you upstairs." I follow her up the stairs.

****

Later that evening, we just finished dinner. Luisa and I clean up the dishes. Rey and Paul discuss Rey's plans for teaching. I can tell Paul is very proud of Rey. Luisa and I bring the dessert to the table, and we all dig into the peach cobbler. After a few minutes, I look over at Rey and he nods at me.

"Paul and Luisa, I need to tell you both something." They both direct their attention to me.

"Go ahead, Kat. You know you can tell us anything," Paul says and Luisa smiles at me. She places her hands in her lap and waits.

"This is very hard for me to say because the last thing I ever want to do is disappoint you." I take a deep breath. I look at Rey and he gives me a small smile, so I continue. "I can't have any more children. After the accident, my uterus had to be removed due to injuries." I watch their faces and they don't look shocked or surprised by what I just said. "I'm so sorry I can't give you grandchildren."

"Kat, honey, you haven't disappointed us," Luisa says. "If I were in your shoes, I wouldn't have any more children even if I could. No mother should ever have to endure what you did. I couldn't do it again." She stands and pulls me into a tight hug. I can't help the tears falling down my face. "You're an amazingly strong woman and I'm proud of who you are. I love you and it doesn't matter to me that I won't have grandchildren. I won't lie to you; I would love one or two but I'm not dying inside about it. I'm happy you both finally found each other and that you'll be close by." She pulls back and looks at me. She gives me a smile through her tears and wipes my tears away. She looks at Paul and I follow her gaze.

"Kids are great, but I'm too old," Paul says, and we all laugh. Luisa throws a napkin at him. A wide grin spreads across his face. "In all seriousness, I'm just happy you're both here and together. Life sucks sometimes but everything happens for a reason. It wasn't fair what happened to you, dear, and I agree with Luisa. Even if you could have children, I wouldn't blame you for not wanting more. I couldn't endure what you did. I'm in awe of you." He stands and opens his arms to me. "Come here, sweet girl."

I walk into his arms. Tears fall in streams. I can't stop them. We stay like that for a minute and soon I feel two more sets of arms come around me. It's the best group hug ever. I laugh when I feel them.

When we break apart, I excuse myself and go to the bathroom. I splash cold water on my face. I wipe my face and when I look up, Rey is standing there.

"Are you okay?"

"Yes. You know you have amazing parents, right?" I say.

"I know. They're pretty special." He has a wide smile on his face.

I take his hand and we head back to the table. We finish dessert and decide to play some cards.

Chapter 39

Kat

Two hours later, I place my cards down and yawn. It's been a long day and I'm exhausted.

"I'm tired. I'm going to call it a night," I say and stand.

"Me, too," Luisa says and stands as well. Paul looks at Rey.

"A couple more rounds, son?" he asks.

"Sure, Dad," Rey says and stands. He kisses his mom's cheek and comes over to me. He takes me into his arms and gives me a gentle kiss. "Good night, baby. I'll be up soon."

"Take your time. Enjoy some time with your dad." I look at Paul. "Good night."

"Good night. Sleep well." I nod and thank him. Luisa and I head upstairs.

I give Luisa a hug when we get to the room we're staying in. I wish her a good night and retreat into the room. I shut the door and lean against the door. I feel so drained yet like a weight is lifted off my shoulders. I flip the switch and the light illuminates the room. I head into the bathroom and turn on the water in the shower. I undress and take a quick shower.

A few minutes later, I towel off and wrap myself in the towel. I brush my teeth with the new toothbrushes Luisa put in the bathroom. I go back into the room and grab my bag. I find my pajamas and put them on. When I look up, my eyes landed on the dresser, and an idea hit me. I open one of the drawers. There are some of Rey's t-shirts and shorts in there. I look through them and pick one of the shirts. I remove my pajamas and slip on one of the t-shirts. It falls to mid-thigh and it's very comfortable. It smells like him. I just found a new nightshirt. I smile, put my pajamas back in my bag, and climb into bed. I turn off the light and try to get some sleep.

****

Rey

A while later, my father and I finish our game. We turn off all the lights, check all the doors, and head off to bed. When I get to my bedroom door, I open it slowly, so I don't wake Kat. I close the door just as slowly and tiptoe to the bathroom. I take a quick shower and dry off. I wrap the towel around my waist and brush my teeth.

I turn off the light and walk back into the bedroom. I go to the bed, drop the towel on the floor, and climb in. I slowly turned toward Kat and put my arm around her. I feel her grab my hand and pull it up toward her breasts.

"I missed you." I hear her say and I smile.

"What are you doing awake?" I snuggle my front to her back.

"I can't sleep without you next to me," she says as she brings my hand to her mouth. I feel her place a kiss on my thumb.

"I can't sleep without you next to me either." I kiss her shoulder. She turns toward me and kisses me.

"I need you." She says, and I lose all control. I kiss her fiercely. There's no way I can stop myself now. I make sure I put as much love into the kiss as possible. I love her so much and I always want her to feel it.

I make love to her slowly and passionately. I make sure she knows she's loved, wanted, and cherished. She deserves all the love I have to give and vow to always make sure she always knows how I feel about her.

Chapter 40

Kat

The next morning, Rey and I drive into downtown Asheville to meet the realtor. We agreed to meet with her at Café Latte. While we're waiting for her, we get coffees and sit outside to watch the locals. It's fun to people-watch in this city. There are so many different types of people here. We also take in the shops, other cafés, art galleries, and bars. From what I can tell, beer is my favorite alcoholic beverage here. Almost every bar has a brewery. Rey's very much into that and we decide to come down on Friday night to check out the nightlife.

A few minutes later, Rose walks up and shakes both our hands.

"Are you ready to find your dream home?" she asks us with a big smile. She's an older woman with a great smile. She's wearing a brown skirt to her knees, a plain white blouse, and brown heels. She's professional and kind. I like her right away and know we made the right decision in going with her.

"Yes, ma'am," I say.

"Great! I have three houses to show you today but the first one just came on the market yesterday. It has everything you're looking for on paper. I'm excited to see it myself." She tells us.

"Sounds great! Can I get you a cup of coffee before we go?" Rey offers.

"No, thank you," Rose replies. "Ready to go?"

We nod and follow her to her car. We climb in and are on our way toward the house.

****

As we approach the first house, I notice how beautiful it is. It's a beige house with a three-car garage. The landscape is pristine and looks professionally done. I immediately notice the view all around the house. It has spectacular mountain views from every angle. The house sits all alone in a cul-de-sac. The closest neighbor is about half a mile away. I look at Rey. He smiles at me, and we climb out of the car. Rose hands me a folder with information on all the houses we are scheduled to see today. Rose walks us to the front door and gives a quick synopsis of the house.

"This house is a custom-built home. It was built two years ago, and the owners are selling it because they got a new job in New York. It's a four-bedroom, three-bath home with a three-car garage. It has a gourmet kitchen and an oversized deck in the backyard. The house sits on a 2-acre property with a pool. It has hardwood floors throughout." Rose unlocks and opens the door. She steps back for Rey and me to go inside first. We step over the threshold and my mouth drops open. The whole back of the house has floor-to-ceiling breathtaking views of the western mountains. It's the most beautiful view I've ever seen.

I look around and it's an open floor plan. From the front door, I can see the dining room and family room, with a fireplace, and part of the kitchen. The hardwood floors are a plank of dark wood, and the walls are off-white. I grab Rey's hand and squeeze. He smiles at me, and we step in and start to look through the house. When we walk around the corner and I see the kitchen, I stop breathing for a second. It's spectacular. It has espresso-colored cabinets with beige-colored matching granite. It's a gourmet kitchen with stainless steel appliances. The sink is located in the center island with a view of the windows. The natural light here is unbelievable.

The master bedroom and bathroom are located on one side of the house. It's huge with its sitting area and fireplace. It has two big walk-in closets that are organized with drawers and center islands. The master bathroom is almost as big as the bedroom. It has double sinks that sit on opposite sides of the bathroom. The toilet sits in a private room. The Jacuzzi tub is in the center of the bathroom with tiled steps on either side. Behind the tub is a large glass stone window. On either side of the tub is an entrance to the shower which is directly behind the tub. There are two shower heads and a huge rain shower head hanging from the ceiling. It's amazing.

Rey walks over to me and places his arms around me. He bends down to whisper in my ear.

"I want to get you in that shower," he says, and I smile.

"It's a beautiful shower," I whisper back.

"I don't give a damn how beautiful it is. I'm imagining how beautiful you would look in that shower," he whispers back, and I can feel the blush come across my face as I look up at him. He groans and kisses me. "Let's go see the rest of our house."

I smile at him, and he leads me back to the main area where we go take a look at the other three bedrooms and two bathrooms. One bathroom is for the other rooms and the other bathroom is a cabana bath that serves as a guest bathroom and a pool bathroom.

We go out onto the deck and look at the backyard. The landscaping in the back is just as pristine as the front. The pool has a breathtaking waterfall. The deck has a separate section for the grill and is completely set up for entertaining. I look back out at the yard. In the far corner of the property, there's a bench swing hanging from a big oak tree's branch. I love that.

"So, tell me what you think of this house," Rose says.

Rey and I look at each other and I nod at him. He turns to Rose.

"We want to make an offer." Rose smiles at his words.

"Are you sure you don't want to look at the other houses?" she asks.

"We're positive," we say, almost in unison.

"Great! Let's go inside and draw up an offer." We follow her back inside. Now, we wait.

Chapter 41

Kat

A few hours later, Rey and I are sitting at a local sports bar having lunch. We decided to go have lunch somewhere that had TVs so we could be distracted while we waited for Rose's call. She told us to go have lunch because she expected to get information on our offer very quickly. The sellers want to sell fast.

I look up at Rey and see he's staring at me.

"What's wrong? Do I have something on my face?" I ask wiping my face with my napkin. He laughs.

"No, baby. I was just thinking about how far we've come in such a short time." He takes a deep breath. "If someone would've told me a year ago that I would be here with you and putting an offer in on a house, I would've laughed in their face."

"I know. I was thinking the same thing last night when I was waiting for you to come to bed. I know things are moving fast but I feel like it's all the right moves," I say.

"Me, too," he says, and his phone starts ringing. He picks up the phone and checks the screen. "It's Rose," he answers.

I wait patiently as I watch him listen to what Rose is saying. A minute later, he thanks her and tells her we'll be in touch. He hits the end button and looks at me.

"Tell me." The look on his face doesn't give anything away. Then, he smiles a big smile and takes my hand.

"They accepted our offer."

I jumped off my chair and say, "Yes!"

He laughs and stands. I fly into his arms; he spins me around and kisses me.

"What's next?" I ask.

"Rose is setting up inspections for next week and getting the title company working as quickly as possible so we can close in two weeks." He tells me as we sit back down.

"That's awesome!" I say. "Once we have an exact closing date, we get to go furniture shopping!"

He waves over the waitress. Once he pays for our meal, we head out and back to Rey's parents' house.

****

Three weeks later, we closed on our home, moved in, and all the furniture has been delivered. The book I started working on in Portugal has been published and the next one is due to be published in a month. I have one more book to be published by the end of the year. I'm working on the Florida book signing for the beginning of the year. Rey got a job as a professor at the University of North Carolina teaching forensics. He's teaching two classes twice a week at the university and teaching an online class. He's been working for the past two weeks and he's loving it. I'm so very proud of him. He was persistent and achieved what he wanted.

My office is one of the rooms that face the back of the house. I made sure I had the mountain views since I love looking at our backyard. My desk is L-shaped, and I'm working toward the side that gives me the views. I put up shelves on both sides of the room. The shelves are still empty. I need to stock them and put up some pictures. I love my office and love working there. For some unknown reason, I'm inspired there.

It's Saturday morning and I'm laying in bed, thinking. I smile. I'm so happy. Things have been going great and I have Rey. He's amazing, and my heart explodes with love for him. I hear him in the kitchen and, within a few seconds, he's walking through the door with a tray in his hands. He's wearing black boxer briefs and nothing else. He looks sexy as hell. The butterflies in my stomach take off as I watch him walk over to me with that amazing smile. He places the tray in front of me.

"Enjoy, my love," he says and leans down. He kisses me, and I hear a low moan rumble in my chest. He pulls away and looks at me. "Don't do that or I will attack you." I laugh but he doesn't crack a smile. "I'm serious, baby. You know how it drives me crazy when you make those noises."

"I know. Maybe I make those noises on purpose." I wink at him. He laughs and kisses me again. When he pulls away, I say "Thank you for breakfast. It looks great. Join me?" Rey walks around the bed and sits next to me.

We eat and talk about our plans for the day. I have some errands to run and Rey's going to work around the yard to prepare it for winter. We finish our breakfast, get up, and head into our shower. We make love in the shower and get on with the rest of our day. It's a great way to start the day. Everyone should start their day this way. Productivity isn't a problem when your day starts like that.

Chapter 42

Rey

I've just finished mowing the lawn and cleaning up. I removed all the summer flowers that will be dying soon. I prepared the landscaping for the fall and winter. I cleaned the pool and spent my Saturday morning doing yard work. I love doing yard work. It clears my head. I used to help my father with his yard. I finally get to work on my own house. I can't seem to get this goofy smile off my face. I'm so incredibly happy. Every single one of my dreams has come true and it's because of Kat. She makes me so happy and life with her is just plain awesome.

I find myself trying to find different ways to romance her. I love being spontaneous and doing special things for her. Her reactions to all those things I do make my insides melt and I nearly drop to my knees. She's an amazing inspiration and I admire everything about her.

I turn on the sprinklers and head inside to take a shower. I walk to the kitchen and pull a bottle of water out of the refrigerator. It isn't overly hot out but warm. The nights are getting cooler. I drink the whole bottle of water in one shot. I throw the bottle in the trash bin and walk into our bedroom. I smile as I look at the perfectly made bed. My beautiful OCD angel. I walk into the closet, pull some clothes out of the drawers, and head into the bathroom. I undress and am about to get into the shower when my cell phone rings. I quickly walk back to the counter and pick up the phone.

"Hello."

"Mr. Vaz?" A male voice asks.

"Yes."

"This is Officer John Mullins," he says, and my heart starts pounding. "I'm calling about Katarina Rodrigues. She was involved in a car accident this morning." I start dressing before he finishes the sentence.

"Is she okay?" I yell into the phone and run out of the bathroom.

"She was transported to Mission St. Joseph's Hospital with some injuries. I can't say the extent of her injuries nor her condition." He informs me.

I run into the kitchen, grab my keys and wallet, and head to the garage.

"Thank you, sir. I'm on my way to the hospital."

"Drive safe, Mr. Vaz," he says, and the line goes dead.

I've never driven so fast in my life. My heart's pounding in my ears and I can't get to the hospital fast enough. I can't stop praying either. *Please God, let her be okay. I can't lose her again. She's been my whole life.*

Five minutes later, I speed into the hospital parking lot and find a spot. I run into the hospital and up to the nurse's desk.

"I'm looking for Katarina Rodrigues," I say loudly. Three nurses turn to look at me. One walks up to me and looks at the computer screen.

"Room 117." I take off running down the hall.

I find her room and take a deep breath before going in. I step in and peek behind the closed curtain. I take in a sharp breath when I see her. Her left cheek is badly bruised. Her left arm is in a sling. She has a bandage on the left side of her forehead and an IV hooked up to her right hand. Her eyes are closed and there's a machine beeping. I walk up to her and lean in to get close to her ear.

"Baby, I'm here," I tell her. Nothing. No movement. She doesn't open her eyes.

The nurse walks in and smiles at me. "Are you Kat's boyfriend?"

"Yes. I'm Rey."

"She's been asking for you," she says.

"Why isn't she waking up?" I ask and look at Kat.

"She came into the ER unconscious but woke up after about ten minutes. Her left shoulder was dislocated so the Doctor had to set it. She was in a lot of pain, so the doctor prescribed a pain killer which made her sleep." She tells me. "Mr. Rey, you can breathe. She's going to be fine. She's just a little banged up."

I take a deep breath and nod. "Thank you."

"You're welcome. I'm going to call the Doctor and let him know you're here so he can speak to you." She walks out of the room.

I sit next to Kat and drop my head. *Thank you, God.*

****

An hour later, Kat is still sleeping, and I haven't moved from the chair I'm sitting in. A very tall man walks in. He's very thin with a mustache. He's wearing a white coat and I assume he's the doctor. I stand to greet him.

"Hi, I'm Dr. Sloan." He extends his hand and I shake it.

"Rey," I say and look at Kat. He walks over to her left side and looks at her.

"Rey, when she came in, she was unconscious. She woke up about ten minutes after she was brought in. I asked her a few questions and she answered them all correctly. I ordered a CT scan just to be on the safe side. She has a very mild concussion but nothing to be concerned with. Her left arm was dislocated, and I had to reset it. Hence why her arm is in a sling. I want her to exercise the arm but to keep it in the sling for about a week. The bruise on her cheek concerned me but all the bones in her face are intact. She has minor cuts and scrapes and more bruises all along her left side. Her leg has another ugly bruise, but nothing's broken. I gave her a strong pain killer and it made her sleep. When she wakes up, she'll be in and out of sleep for another two hours. We'll be giving her a much lower dose of a painkiller from then on. I gave her something strong so her body would relax. She was experiencing pain all over her body and she seemed so agitated. She'll be achy for the next couple of days. None of her injuries are life-threatening. I want to keep her overnight for observation and she'll be able to go home tomorrow." Dr. Sloan says with a smile.

"Thank you," I tell him and take a deep breath.

"You're welcome. I'll come by tomorrow morning to see her and do her discharge papers. If you need anything until then, the nurse knows how to reach me."

"Thank you so much." We shake hands again.

"No problem. You take care and I'll see you in the morning." He leaves the room.

I lean down and kiss her cheek. The doors open again, and a police officer is standing there.

"Mr. Vaz?" He asks.

"Yes, sir."

"I'm Officer Mullins. We spoke on the phone earlier." He walks further into the room until he's standing at the foot of Kat's bed.

"Yes. Thank you for calling me." We shake hands and I wait for him to continue.

"How's she doing?"

"She's doing well. It's nothing life-threatening. She'll be going home tomorrow if all goes well tonight." I look at Kat.

"That's great to hear. She's very lucky. When I came upon the accident, I expected to see worse."

"Can you tell me what happened?" I ask him.

"She was T-boned when some guy took a red light. With more investigation, we found out he was high on cocaine. He walked away without a scratch on him. Unfortunately, the stupid walk away and the innocent get hurt." He shakes his head.

"Please tell me I never have to see this guy because I'll kill him," I say through gritted teeth.

"No, sir. The state is filing charges and Ms. Rodrigues will not need to appear because she was injured. You don't need to worry about it. He'll be in jail for a long time," he says. I nod, and he continues. "I came to check on Ms. Rodrigues and to bring you a copy of the report. You'll need to file a claim with your insurance company. His insurance information is on there too and I suggest you call them as well."

"Thank you, Officer. I'll do that right away."

The Officer gives me all the information as to where Kat's car is and he's pretty sure it's a total loss. Once he's done, he shakes my hand and leaves. I call both insurance companies and get the claim information. Once I'm done, I sit and wait for the love of my life to wake up.

Chapter 43

Kat

I wake up and immediately feel the pain. *What the hell?* My body aches and my arm throbs. I look around and see Rey sleeping in the chair. His head is in an awkward position. His neck is going to kill him.

"Rey." He sits up quickly. He smiles when he sees I'm awake. He stands and comes to stand next to me.

"Hey, baby. How are you feeling?"

"My body aches," I tell him. "But one part of my body aches the most."

"Which one is that? I'll get the nurse. She can tell the doctor." He starts to move, and I grab his hand. He stops and looks at me.

"No one can heal this ache but you," I tell him, and he smiles at me. He moves closer to me, leans down, and gently kisses my lips. "I feel so much better now." He laughs and pulls the chair closer to the bed.

"I'm glad you're okay. I nearly had a heart attack when I got the phone call from the police." I see his eyes swell with tears.

"I'm sorry I scared you."

"It wasn't your fault. I just thank God you're okay." I look at him, sober now, and I feel the tears swell in my eyes.

"Why do terrible things keep happening to us?" I ask him. He looks at me as a tear falls down my cheek. He wipes the tear away with his thumb.

"Oh, baby, I don't know. I wish I had the answer to that question."

"I'm just so scared bad things will continue to happen, and we're torn apart." I shake my head to get rid of the ugly thought. "I'm sorry. I shouldn't have asked that question. I need to keep a positive attitude. I can't go back to that dark place."

"Sweetheart, look at me." Rey stands and places his hands on either side of my face. "We need to remain strong. We can get through anything. I'm pretty sure we've already proved that." He kisses me gently. "I love you so much."

"I love you." I give him a weak smile.

"Are you hungry?" he asks. "The nurse said you can have anything you want."

"Yes, I am actually. Why don't you surprise me?"

"You got it." He kisses me again and heads to the door. "I'll be right back."

"Rey?" I call after him.

"Yes," he says as he turns to look at me.

"Be careful."

"Always." He winks at me.

He walks out, and the door closes behind him. I lean my head back and close my eyes. *Please God, watch over us. I can't handle it if I lose him, too.*

****

The next afternoon, I'm released from the hospital. We pick up my pain meds and go home. We walk into the kitchen, and I sit at the table. Rey gets me a glass of water and my pain pill. I thank him and take the pill. I look outside and see all the work he did. The yard looks great.

"The yard looks great!" I tell him as he comes to sit next to me.

"Thanks," he says. "Do you want to go lay down?"

"I think I want to sit in my chair in our bedroom and do some reading." My chair's a comfy oversized recliner. Rey and I decided to put recliners in our sitting area.

"I'll grab your tablet." He goes to my office as I head into our bedroom.

I sit down in my chair and throw a blanket over my legs. Rey walks in and hands me the tablet. "Enjoy, baby. Let me know if you need me." He kisses me softly.

"Why don't you take a nap? You haven't slept, and I know you're tired."

"I'm good. There's something I need to do and then make us dinner," he says and heads toward the door. He stops and looks at me. "Do you realize how beautiful you look?"

"Are you kidding? I'm battered, bruised, and swollen. Like that's sexy, but I love you for saying it." I laugh. He stares at me.

"I'm not kidding and I'm not trying to make you feel better. You do look beautiful. You will always be beautiful, no matter what." He walks back over to me. When he reaches me, he drops to his knees and takes my hand. "You're the most beautiful woman I've ever laid eyes on. Every time I look at you, I stop breathing. I can't believe you're mine. You amaze me, and I cherish you."

At this point, tears are falling like waterfalls again. He's so sweet and so romantic. I don't know what to say to that. I'm speechless.

"Don't cry. It kills me when I see you cry." He wipes the tears from my face.

"Thank you, baby. I love you." I manage to get out and he smiles.

"I love you, too. Rest now." He stands and walks out of the room. I compose myself and close my eyes. I think of my family. They're my guardian angels. I smile at the thought and start reading my book.

Chapter 44

Rey

When I walked into Kat's office earlier, I noticed she hadn't put any pictures on the wall yet and the shelves were still empty. I decided to jumpstart the process with a few ideas I had.

I walk into my office and sit down in front of my laptop. I research my ideas and find what I'm looking for. I order everything I want and check on my online class. I answer a few emails and move my laptop to the side. I grab my briefcase and remove a folder. I open it and start to grade some papers. I need to get all these papers graded by Monday.

My mind wanders, and I can't concentrate. I only have one thing on my mind, and I need to take care of it as soon as possible. I place the laptop in front of me again and I look up the local jewelry store. I look through their inventory and make a mental note of what I want to see. I call the store and make an appointment for tomorrow afternoon to buy Kat's engagement ring. Marrying her is my dream and now it'll be a reality. Now, I need to think of the perfect way to ask her. No more wasting time.

****

The next afternoon, Kat decides to take a nap. I let her know I'm going to run some errands before she falls asleep. I make sure she gets into bed okay, kiss her, and leave. I'm on my way to the jewelry store. I hope I can find what I have in mind for her. She deserves only the very best.

I get to the jewelry store and find a spot right in front. I park and head in. When I walk in, I'm greeted by an older woman with grey hair and a dark grey suit.

"Can I help you, sir?" she asks.

"Yes, ma'am. I have a two o'clock appointment."

"Are you Rey?"

"Yes, ma'am," I respond.

"Wonderful. Come with me. Your appointment is with Rick." She leads me to the back of the store. A young man's standing behind the counter. He smiles as I walk up.

"Rick, this is Rey," she introduces us and walks away.

"Hi, Rey." Rick extends his hand to me. We shake.

"Hi."

"Let's go over here and get started." Rick walks over to another counter. When I look down, there are a lot of rings. I'm suddenly feeling overwhelmed. I have no idea what I'm going to choose. "Do you know what you're looking for?"

"I thought I did until I just looked down." He laughs.

"I understand. Hopefully, I'll be some help to you."

"I hope so," I say and look down again.

Rick asks me a few questions about the cut, color, and size I need. Based on my answers, he takes a few rings out of the case and shows them to me individually. I look at them but none of them appeals to me. After I look at all the rings Rick shows me, I decide to look back into the case. I look through all the rings. Once I'm about to give up, I see it. It's sitting by itself in the upper right-hand corner of the case. I point at it.

"Can I please see that one?" Rick looks down and smiles.

"Absolutely." He reaches into the case. He pulls it out and places it on the counter. He removes it from the box and hands it to me. I look at it and I see it on Kat's finger. It's the perfect ring.

"This is it," I tell Rick. He nods his understanding.

"Great!" he says. "Let me tell you a little about the ring. It's a princess-cut two-carat diamond. It's set in platinum with two small diamonds on either side of the main diamond. It's a total of three carats."

"How much?" I ask.

"It's twenty thousand dollars, sir," Rick answers with a smile.

"How long will it take to get it sized?" I continue to look at the ring.

"Let me check the size of the ring but it usually takes two days." I hand him the ring. He sizes the ring and looks up. He smiles at me. "This is the perfect ring because it happens to be the exact size you need."

A huge smile spreads across my face. "I'll take it." There's no price tag when it comes to my girl.

Ten minutes later, I'm walking out of the jewelry store with Kat's ring in my pocket and headed home.

Chapter 45

Kat

Two weeks have passed since my accident. My face and arm are healing nicely. All my other cuts and bruises are pretty much gone now. I finally get clearance from my doctor this morning to resume normal activities. I'm relieved because I'm dying to be with Rey. He's so afraid to hurt me that he barely touches me.

I park my car in the garage and smile when I see Rey's already home from teaching his class. I quickly get out and head inside. When I walk inside, I call out for Rey. He comes out of the hallway that leads to our offices smiling. He walks up to me, takes me into his arms, and kisses me so passionately.

"Wow!" I say, and he laughs.

"Hi, baby."

"Hi." I'm still breathless from his kiss.

"What did the doctor say?"

"All clear to resume normal activities." I give him a huge grin and wiggle my eyebrows.

"Thank God. The last two weeks have dragged." He takes a deep breath and runs his hand through his hair.

"I know." I bring my arms up, lock them behind his neck, and pull him to me. "Make love to me," I say, just as our lips are about to touch. He moans and brings me closer to him.

"Oh, I will, baby, but first I need to show you something." He leads me to my office. The door is closed, and he places me in front of the door. I look behind me and raise my eyebrows. I open the door slowly and we walk in.

I go to the middle of the room and stop dead in my tracks. My hand comes up to my mouth and the tears immediately start to fall. I can't believe what I'm seeing. I turn and look at Rey. He's standing at the door, watching me. There are two canvas portraits on the wall on either side of my desk. One is of my children and the other one is of me and Rey. The picture of my kids is the last portrait taken of them and our picture was taken of us at a wedding in Portugal. Both portraits are gorgeous.

I walk up to one of my children. I run my fingers on the canvas and my heartaches. I miss them so much. The hurt gets better with time but missing them only gets stronger and stronger as the days pass. I look at their beautiful faces and a sob escapes my lips. I would do anything to bring my angels back. I feel Rey's hands on my shoulders. I turn and fall into his arms. I instantly feel better.

"Thank you so much. I love them."

"Are you sure, baby? I don't want to make this harder on you." I can hear the uncertainty in his voice. "I thought this would be nice but if it's too hard, I completely understand."

"It's perfect. I do love them. I just miss them so much and every day that goes by makes me miss them more and more." I move my head so I can look at him. "Thank you."

"My pleasure. I wish I could take your pain away. What happened to you isn't fair." He smiles at me and gives me a soft kiss. His lips felt so good on mine. "Look at your bookshelves."

I move away from him, get closer to my bookshelves, and gasp.

"Oh, wow! This is unbelievable!" I walk over to one of the shelves and pick up one of the canvas pictures sitting on a stand. It's the cover of my first published book. He's made a canvas print of all the covers of my published books and set them on the shelves sitting on a stand. Each shelf has a cover yet there's still plenty of room for other books.

"This is an amazing idea! How did you think of this?"

"When I came in here the other day to grab your tablet, I noticed how bare it was and decided to perk it up a bit. I went online to get an enlargement made of some of your photos and saw the canvas print options. I thought those would look great in here. Once I ordered those pictures, I thought of this idea." He points to the book covers. "You didn't have anything anywhere showing your work, so I thought this would look great on your bookshelves." He walks over to my desk and picks up two framed 5x7 pictures and hands them to me. I look down at them. One is a group picture of my parents, me, my husband, and my children. This specific picture of my family was taken the night before they died at a function we attended. It's the perfect picture for my desk. The other picture is of Rey. I took that picture of him when we first moved into the house. He's staring out at the mountains with a small smile on his face. He looks unbelievably sexy, and he knows how much I love that picture. "I hope you like them."

"It's all perfect! Thank you so much!" I throw my arms around him. I hug him tightly. "I love you so much."

"I love you," he says. "I only want to see you happy. Your smile lights up a room and I always want to see it. Your tears gut me."

He kisses the top of my head, and we head out of the office to make dinner.

Chapter 46

Kat

I wake up early today, take a quick shower, and throw on a pair of sweatpants and a t-shirt. I throw my hair into a ponytail as I head into the kitchen to start baking. First things first, I start a pot of coffee. Today is Thanksgiving and we're hosting. I'm excited about this year's holidays. Although I'll miss my family like crazy and there will be many times of sadness, it's the first time in years I feel like celebrating. Rey's parents are coming over. Uncle Manny and Aunt Lina are coming up too. They're staying with Paul and Luisa for the holidays.

I'm working on the pumpkin pie crust when Rey walks into the kitchen. I smile at him as he comes over to kiss me. He turns and pours two cups of coffee. He places one of the cups next to me and leans up against the counter to watch me.

"Do you need some help?" he asks.

"No, thanks. I've got it."

"I want to help with something." He watches me start the pie filling. "Are you making pumpkin pie from scratch?"

"Yes, I am." I look at him and his face lights up.

"That's incredible. I can't wait to taste it. I've only had store-bought. No one has ever bothered to make one from scratch."

"I've always made it from scratch," I tell him. "I'm going to make an apple pie from scratch next."

"Seriously?" He puts his hands up to his heart. "You're going to kill me."

"I always make these two pies on Thanksgiving. Most people like pumpkin pie but some don't. So, I always have both pies." I fill the pie shell and put it in the oven. I wash my hands and wipe them. I pick up the coffee cup and take a sip. "Do you want to help me with the apple pie?"

"I would love to." He places his coffee mug down and proceeds to wash his hands as I put away the pumpkin pie ingredients and take out the apple pie ingredients.

"First, we have to peel and cut up all the apples." I place the apples on the counter and take out two lemons. I pick an apple out of the bag and show him how to peel and cut up the apple. We peel and cut as we discuss the menu. Rey's eyes light up as I tell him how I'm going to prepare the turkey and all the sides.

Once the apples are peeled, I roll two lemons on the counter, cut them in half, and squeeze the juice over the apples. I mix them and set the bowl aside.

"I didn't realize apple pie had lemon in it," Rey says, and I smile at him. It's so cute how he doesn't know what the lemon is for.

"The lemon is only to stop the apples from turning brown." He shakes his head and watches as I bring the food processor over to the island. I put flour, sugar, and cubed butter in the food processor and hit the pulse button. Once it's the consistency I'm looking for, I sprinkle a little flour on the counter. I take the lid off the processor and dump the contents on the floured counter. I flour the rolling pin and hand it to Rey. He smiles and starts rolling out the dough.

****

Paul leans back in his chair and pats his belly. He places his napkin on the table and picks up his wine glass.

"Kat, I always thought my wife's Thanksgiving dinner was amazing. I must say yours is a very close second. That was a great meal. I'm stuffed." Paul smiles at me. Everyone at the table murmurs their agreement. I'm pleased everyone enjoyed the meal.

"Thanks, everyone. I hope you're not too full. I have pumpkin pie and apple pie," I say as I stand up to start clearing the dishes. Rey takes my hand.

"Sit back down, sweetheart. You've been on your feet all day preparing this meal. I'll take care of the dishes," he says and kisses the top of my head as he stands.

"No, you don't." Luisa stands. "Rey, sit down and relax. I'll clean." She begins grabbing plates and heading toward the kitchen.

"I'll help." Aunt Lina stands and grabs some plates too.

I stand and smile at Rey. "I'm going to get the coffee started." He nods, and I walk into the kitchen with some dishes.

"Didn't I tell you I would clean up?" Luisa takes the dishes from me.

"Yes, but I want to get the coffee started. I wasn't going to come in here empty-handed." I say, smiling at her. She laughs and shakes her head. "Thank you for your help."

"My pleasure, dear." She pats my cheek.

I start the coffee and uncover the pies sitting on the center island. Both women compliment how the pies look as I pull out plates, forks, and coffee cups.

"Thank you. The pies are my Thanksgiving tradition. I haven't made them in five years, and it felt good making them again. I hadn't realized how much I missed making them." My eyes swell with tears.

Aunt Lina takes my hand and gives me a small smile. "Is this the first holiday you've celebrated since the accident?"

I nod as the tears fall from my eyes. She embraces me, and I feel Luisa come and hug the two of us. That makes me giggle and we start laughing. When we pull apart, all three of us are wiping our eyes.

Rey walks into the kitchen at that moment. He stops dead in his tracks and stares at us.

"Is everything okay?"

"Yes," Luisa says. "We just had an emotional moment." She walks back to the sink to finish loading the dishwasher. I smile at Rey, and he flashes me the sexy smile that always makes my legs go weak. He comes up to me and takes the plates and forks from me. He leans in and places his lips to my ear.

"Are you sure you're okay?" he whispers.

"Yes, I promise," I whisper back. He nods and heads back into the dining room. I follow him with coffee cups and spoons. I walk back into the kitchen to get the cream, sugar, and pot of coffee. Aunt Lina and Luisa each grab a pie and we head back to the table.

Chapter 47

Kat

We decide to have dessert around the fire pit. Rey started it while we were cleaning up the dishes. Each one of us makes our plates, grabs our coffee, and heads outside. It is a chilly night but not so cold we can't enjoy being outside. We're sitting and having small talk when Rey abruptly stands.

"There's something I need to say." He moves my chair back a little, so I can look at him. He smiles and winks at me. "I want to thank you, Mom, Dad, Uncle Manny, and Aunt Lina for being here tonight. Thank you, my love, for putting together that amazing meal and those even better pies." I laugh. He grins but he suddenly looks nervous. "Baby, you're such an amazing woman. I'll be forever thankful to Uncle Manny for throwing us together. I thank God every day we made our way to each other. Thank you for loving me and for giving me the chance to love you. Loving you has been such an incredible journey and I hope I can enjoy it for many more years to come." I look around. Aunt Lina and Luisa are crying. Uncle Manny and Paul both have goofy smiles on their faces. I giggle and turn back to Rey only to find him down on one knee in front of me. I gasp and stare at him. He pulls a small box from his pocket, opens it, and holds it out toward me. My eyes are locked on his face. I don't even look at what's in the box. I stare at him, mouth open. "Kat, will you do me the honor of becoming my wife?"

I continue to stare at him. He stares back at me. After a long moment, he leans in. "Please answer me," he whispers. "I'm getting nervous now." I blink and slowly smile at him. I look down at the ring and let out another gasp. It's huge and unbelievably gorgeous. My eyes go back up to lock on his. I finally find my voice.

"Yes, of course, I will."

He lets out the breath he was holding and pulls the ring out of the box. He takes my left hand and places the ring on my finger. He stands, and I fling myself into his arms. Everyone claps as we kiss. He kisses me so passionately I feel my legs giving out underneath me. He holds me tighter and pulls away. "I love you."

"I love you." We turn to our family.

All four of them stand quickly and head over to us. Hugs are exchanged all around and the ladies are going crazy over the ring. I can't believe how gorgeous it is. He spent an unnecessary fortune when I only need him. I look at him and he winks. I feel my face flush and continue my conversation with the ladies.

Paul clears his throat and, when I turn, I see a bottle of champagne in his hands. "I want to make a toast," he says and pops the top of the bottle. Everyone cheers as he pours the champagne into the glasses Rey brought out. Each person takes a glass and Rey walks over to me. He places an arm around my waist, and I do the same to him.

"Rey, your mother, and I are so happy to see you found your happiness. You've made us so proud of the man you are. You're an amazing son and we couldn't have asked for a better daughter-in-law. Welcome to our family, Kat. You're an amazing woman and deserve so much happiness. We love you both and wish you many blessings and happiness." Paul raises his glass, and everyone does the same and takes a sip. I walk over to Paul and give him a tight hug.

"Thank you, Paul. It means the world to me that I have you and Luisa as parents-in-law." I step away. He has tears in his eyes and smiles. I smile back, and he quickly looks away. I giggle, and everyone finds their seats again. The wedding talk immediately starts.

"Kat, do you know what kind of wedding you want?" Luisa asks. I smile and look at Rey.

"Rey and I haven't talked about it, but I want something small. I would be happy with just the six of us. I would like a destination wedding with a small ceremony and dinner on the beach. Something very casual would suit me just fine." Rey reaches for my hand.

"I was thinking the same thing. I love the idea. Let's do it." He says, and I laugh.

"Okay. That's settled then. Now, we just have to pick a date."

"New Year's Day," Rey says, and I smile wide.

"I love it." Everyone erupts into chatter for the rest of the night.

Chapter 48

Kat

It's ten when everyone finally leaves and I'm exhausted. It's been the best Thanksgiving ever. I'm so happy, and I feel like I'm floating. I still can't believe I'm engaged to Rey. It's a dream that's come true. I'm removing the tablecloth from the table when the ring catches my eye. I haven't had a chance to look at it since he gave it to me. I bring my hand up and look at the ring. It's stunning and looks great on my finger. Rey went above and beyond with this ring. I'll cherish it as long as I live. I feel Rey come behind me and wrap his arms around my waist.

"The ring is beautiful," I tell him.

"As soon as I saw it, I knew it was yours. It screamed your name." He kisses my cheek.

"I love it and will cherish it as long as I live, but I need to tell you I didn't need a ring like this. I would have been perfectly happy without a ring."

"I know that, but you deserve that ring and so much more."

I turn in his arms and wrap my arms around his neck.

"Thank you." He leans down and kisses me.

The kiss starts slow and soft but quickly turns passionate. He leans down and picks me up without breaking the kiss and walks us into our bedroom. He lies down on the bed and lies next to me. He brushes a strand of hair from my face and just looks at me. I can see so much love in his eyes. It overwhelms me a little.

"I love you."

"I love you. So much so that sometimes my heart hurts," I say.

He nods. "I know the feeling. I feel the same way. I also know I don't deserve your love."

"What? Why would you say that? Of course, you deserve my love. You saved my life. I was slowly making my way into my grave. Day by day, I was deteriorating until you walked back into my life again." I tear falls from my eye. He wipes it away from my cheek with his thumb and kisses me again.

I don't hold anything back with this kiss. I kiss him with so much passion and love and I hope he feels just how I feel about him. I sure as hell feel it from him. He breaks the kiss and looks at me for a moment. I know he had felt what I felt just by the look in his eyes. He slams his lips to mine and before we know it, we're naked.

He kisses every inch of my body. He's driving me crazy. I can't believe how my body responds to his touch. I want him so badly. He's a very thorough lover and I try to be just as thorough with him.

I turn him over and straddle him. I kiss him and move my way to his neck. I work my way all over him and back to his mouth. This time I sink into him and hear him moan. I let out a small gasp. Every time feels like the first time with him. I make love to him slowly until I know we both can't take it anymore. I quicken the pace and we cum together, fast and hard. I collapse on top of him, and we stay like that until we can catch our breaths.

"How is it that it seems to get more amazing?" I ask him.

"I don't know, but it sure as hell does. It's mind-blowing every single time."

I move off him and he pulls me to his side. My head is on his shoulder and my hand sits on his chest. I drape my leg over him, and his hand caresses up and down my side. I smile as I feel myself falling asleep. I dream of marrying the love of my life.

Chapter 49

Kat

I wake up early Christmas morning to make Rey breakfast. I'm so excited about opening presents. I got Rey something he's always wanted but never could have because he was always moving. It was delivered yesterday, and I've had it locked in my office. Before I make breakfast, I get his present ready and put it under the tree. Most of the presents under the tree are gone because we had taken them to Paul and Luisa's last night. We had Christmas Eve dinner and played games. We had so much fun.

I prepare bacon, eggs, and blueberry muffins for breakfast. I put everything on a tray and walk into the bedroom. He's still asleep. I watch him for a minute. He's lying on his back. One of his hands rests on his chest and the other arm is draped across his eyes. He looks so sexy. I lean down and start kissing his chest. I feel him move and look up at him. He's removed his arm from his eyes and is watching me.

"Merry Christmas." I continue kissing my way up. He smiles, and I feel his hand in my hair.

"Merry Christmas," he says as I reach his mouth. I bite down on his lower lip and kiss him slowly. When we break apart, he smiles. "This is an awesome way to wake up."

I laugh as I get the tray of food I placed on the dresser. I wait for him to finish sitting up and set it down in front of him. He looks down at it.

"Damn, baby. This looks delicious." He digs right into it.

"Enjoy it." I walk around the bed and sit next to him. I sip my coffee and take a muffin. A few minutes later, we devoured the whole tray of food and I get up to take the tray. "Time to open presents." I walk out of the room and Rey starts to laugh. I set the tray down on the kitchen counter and walk into the living room. I sit on the floor next to the tree and wait. Rey walks in wearing only a pair of sweatpants. My mouth waters and my stomach does these weird flips at the sight of him. That gorgeous man is all mine. I smile as he sits down next to me.

I pick up the box and set it down in front of him. "Open this one first." I wait patiently. He slowly lifts the lid off the box and looks inside. His head snaps up to look at me. He reaches his hands into the box and pulls out a yellow lab puppy. He looks at him and reads the note attached to his collar, '*Hi Daddy! What's my name* He laughs and looks at me.

"Hey, little guy," he says to the puppy. The puppy tries to lick Rey's face and he laughs. "We're already bonding." He leans in to kiss me. I place both my hands on his face and give him a hard kiss. I pull away and grin.

"When I saw him, I melted. I bought him on the spot, and he was delivered yesterday. He's a good puppy and a very fast learner." I tell him. "All he needs now is a name."

Rey picks him up, so they're nose to nose. He examines him for a moment. "Champ. His name is Champ." I laugh, and he looks at me. "Thank you."

"Champ it is." Rey puts him down on the floor and Champ comes to lay between my legs and closes his eyes.

"Hey Champ, she's mine, man," Rey says, and we both start laughing.

Rey stands, reaches toward the back of the tree, and takes out a small box. He comes back over and sits back down. He hands me the box. "Open yours now."

I take the box from him and open it. I pull out a white gold charm bracelet. It's stunning, and it already has some charms on it. Rey proceeds to explain what each one means.

"The little girl stands for your daughter, the little boy stands for your son, the couple holding the heart stands for your parents, the book stands for your writing, the map of Portugal stands for where we found each other, the heart stands for my heart, and the kissing couple stands for our love." He points to each one of the charms as he explains.

"I love it. Thank you." I extend my wrist toward him, and he puts it on me. I pick up Champ, place him on the floor, and get up on my knees. I hug and kiss Rey for the amazing gift. I sit back down, and we open the rest of our gifts. There are little things like clothing and gift certificates to our favorite stores.

We decide to go hiking in the snow and stop in town for lunch. After lunch, we walk around the city a bit and come home. When we get home, we make love for the rest of the afternoon. It was the perfect Christmas.

Chapter 50

Rey

Four days later, we're on a plane heading toward the Bahamas. We left Champ at home and Katie, our very pregnant neighbor. I already miss the little guy. Tomorrow, my parents, Uncle Manny and Aunt Lina will be heading out. Kat and I have handled the airline tickets and hotel reservations for everyone since we decided to have our wedding out of town. We're just about to land when I feel Kat reach for my hand. I lace my fingers through hers and look at her. She looks out the window. We watch as we land at the North Eleuthera airport in the Bahamas.

A few minutes later, we were walking through the airport toward baggage claim to pick up our bags and catch our ride to The Cove resort. We quickly get our bags and head outside. There's a Range Rover parked outside the airport doors with a man standing next to it. He's holding a sign with my last name printed on it. We walk up to him and introduce ourselves. He loads the luggage in the car and we're on our way.

"Mr. Vaz, I've called and done the automatic check-in. I will stop to pick up the key and will take you directly to your cottage." The driver tells us.

"Thank you, sir." I look at Kat. She has a surprised look on her face and mouths 'Wow' to me. The drive to the resort is short, yet beautiful. The palm trees and the ocean are breathtaking.

We drive up to the front of our cottage and I jump out. I hold out my hand for Kat and she steps out. By the time I turn around, the driver has the door to the cottage open and is taking our luggage inside. He sets the bags down at the front door and hands me the key. I hand him a tip and thank him. He walks out, and I close the door behind him. Kat stands frozen looking at the view.

I follow her eyes and am amazed. It's a breathtaking view of palm trees and crystal-clear water. Directly in front of us are double glass doors leading to a small deck with two lounge chairs. As we step down off the deck, we're standing on our private beach. Off to the right is another small deck with a high-top table and two chairs.

We take a deep breath and walk straight to the water. We take off our shoes and go into the water. It's so warm. I take Kat into my arms and kiss her.

"What an amazing place!" she says. "The private cottage is unreal!" She has a huge smile on her face.

"I'm so glad you like it. This will be our little paradise for the next week." I tell her. Somehow, her smile gets bigger.

"I'm so happy!" She kisses me again.

After a few minutes, we break apart and I lead her back to the cottage where we proceed to look around. It has a private bedroom and bathroom off to the right of the main room. The main room has a TV and a couch. The bedroom has a king-sized bed, a TV on the wall, and a nightstand on either side of the bed. The bed faces a wall of windows with a direct view of the beach. It's going to be a wonderful way to wake up. The best part is the cottage sits by itself. The next cottage available is on the other side of the property so the beach is all ours.

We continue into the bathroom. The double sinks are stainless steel with granite countertops. Sitting on the countertop are full bottles of island shampoo, conditioner, and bubble bath. There's also a bar of island soap sitting in front of them along with a shower cap, a mini sewing kit, Q-tips, and cotton balls. Towels of various sizes hang from a towel rack and a hairdryer is on the wall next to the sinks. We turn to see a huge stand-up shower in the corner with showerheads all around. Right next to it sits a Jacuzzi tub.

"That looks heavenly right now," Kat whispers, smiling at it.

"Let's get unpacked and I'll draw you a nice hot bubble bath." I open another door. It reveals the toilet. I open it wider, so Kat can see, and she laughs.

"That's good to know!" She laughs harder. "I'll take you up on the bath only if you join me."

"Absolutely!" I lead her back into the bedroom. I let go of her hand and get the bags. When I come back in, she's lost in thought looking out toward the ocean. "You okay?" I wrap one arm around her waist and the other around her neck. I kiss her. She immediately places her arms over mine and leans into me. I love when she does that.

"Yes. I was just thanking God for you and how fortunate we've been." She turns her head to look at me. "Let's unpack and get to that bath."

"Amen to that. I've been dying to get you naked," I say, and she giggles.

Chapter 51

Rey

At eleven the next morning, we greet my parents, Uncle Manny, and Aunt Lina in the main hotel lobby. I checked them into the hotel before their arrival and already have their keys in my hand. We escort them to their rooms in the main hotel and we head down to the hotel restaurant for lunch.

While we wait for our meals, Kat's telling them about our cottage and how we've arranged to have our wedding ceremony and reception take place just outside our cottage. We met with the wedding planner this morning and took care of the details. Kat bought her dress in North Carolina and brought it with her. So, it seems, we're completely ready.

"Kat, I have something I would like you to wear tomorrow." My mother says as she reaches into her purse. She pulls out a red velvet box and hands it to her. Kat takes it and opens it slowly. I can see her hands shaking. Kat's hand immediately goes to her mouth, and she looks at my mom with a stunned expression. It's a stand of stunning white pearls. In between each pearl is a small diamond. It's really beautiful. It looks familiar for some reason. I know I've seen the necklace before.

"Luisa, are you sure?" Kat asks.

"Yes. It would be an honor to see you wear it on your wedding day. I never had a daughter of my own and you're like a daughter to me. It'll be your something old. My mother wore it on her wedding day, and I wore it on mine," Mom says. Tears fall down Kat's face. Bingo. I knew I've seen the necklace before. Mom had it on in her wedding pictures.

"It would be an honor," she tells her as she stands and embraces my mother. I'm touched my mother feels that way about my bride. I look at Dad and he has tears in his eyes as he watches Kat. *Softie.* I smile. I know he feels the same way as Mom does about Kat.

"I also have your something borrowed," Mom says as she reaches into her purse again. *The damn thing has no bottom!* Kat laughs as Mom hands her a hairclip. The hairclip has pearls to match the necklace. In the middle of the clip, the letter 'V' is encrusted in rhinestones. "My mother had it made especially for my wedding day."

"Thank you, Luisa. It would be an honor and a pleasure to wear both of these things on my wedding day." Kat says as she wipes the tears from her face.

"I have something blue," Aunt Lina says, and everyone laughs. She reaches into her purse, pulls out a small bag, and hands it to Kat. Kat opens the bag and immediately blushes and starts to laugh. She reaches into the bag and pulls out a light blue garter. The table erupts with laughter. "What?" she says. "It's an important part of the wedding!" She has a sly smile on her face.

"I agree," I say. "It'll be very fun for me." I place my hand out and high-five Aunt Lina. Laughter erupts once again as our food arrives. We eat, have some coffee, and spend the rest of the afternoon relaxing on the beach.

****

Rey

Our wedding day has finally arrived. Kat's still sleeping, and I've been watching her for the last twenty minutes. I hear a knock at the door. I gently maneuver myself out of bed, so I won't wake her and walk to the door. I open it and see the room service I ordered.

I set the tray down on the table and go back into the bedroom to wake my sleeping beauty. I sit on the bed next to her and start to kiss her neck. She moves and slowly opens her eyes. A slow smile appears on her lips.

"Good morning, gorgeous," I say, still kissing her neck.

"Good morning, handsome." She let outs a small moan.

I move up to her lips and kiss her. "Breakfast is on the table." I stand, put my hand out, and help her out of bed. She follows me to the table and sits. I uncover the trays and reveal an assortment of muffins and fruit, coffee, and orange juice.

"It looks so good," Kat says and starts to pour us both some coffee.

When I'm about to sit, a knock comes on the door. I open the door. There stands Mom, Dad, Uncle Manny, and Aunt Lina.

"Good morning!" Mom walks in.

"Good morning. What are you doing here so early?" I ask them.

"We're here to help Kat get ready and you're going with your father and Uncle Manny to get ready in our room," Mom quickly spits out.

"I know that was the plan, but I was going to go after breakfast," I say as Dad walks up to me and places a hand on my shoulder.

"Son, these women have womanly things to do. Let's go get a man's breakfast and get ready. Let's let them do their thing." He and Uncle Manny nod at me. I look at Kat and she looks as stunned as I do but shrugs her shoulders.

"Okay. Let me get sandals on my feet and my stuff." I walk toward the bathroom.

Five minutes later, we're walking out of the cottage and Mom doesn't even let me kiss Kat goodbye. I'm not very happy right now. I know I'm pouting, and I don't care. The only thing that makes everything better is knowing that in three hours Kat will be my wife. My dream is finally coming true.

Chapter 52

Kat

I look out the cottage window and see Rey heading toward the white arch sitting on the sand. There's a small round table in the middle of the arch. Four chairs sit on the sand directly in front of the arch. The photographer's already snapping photos. He was with me earlier. The ocean is the backdrop, but I can't keep my eyes off Rey. He looks so handsome and utterly sexy. He's wearing a dark grey suit that looks fantastic on him. He's speaking to the notary when I hear Luisa.

"Are you ready?"

"Yes, I am," I say and smile at her.

I grab my bouquet of white roses and head out of the cottage. Everyone takes their seats and I head toward Rey. I wear a simple strapless white dress that fits my curves perfectly. I wear a strand of pearls around my neck and simple diamond studs in my ears. The bracelet Rey gave me for Christmas is on my wrist. I'm wearing my hair half up with the hairclip holding it. The rest of my hair hangs around my shoulders in soft curls, and I have strands of soft curls framing my face. I'm wearing a pair of silver heels on my feet.

I watch Rey as I walk to him. He's not smiling. He's staring at me. I swallow hard and start to panic. *What if he doesn't like what he's seeing?* My heart pounds in my ears. I finally get to him. He leans in toward my ear.

"You look beautiful and unbelievably sexy," he whispers. I blush, and a large smile comes across my lips. My heart instantly calms.

"You look amazing, too," I whisper back, and he straightens. He winks and we both look at the notary. I place my bouquet on the table in front of his paperwork like he asked me to and proceed with the ceremony.

We exchange traditional vows. We decide not to do our own. As special as doing our own would be, we decide we have too much to say, and it would be extremely difficult for both of us. After the vows, we exchange the rings. Rey's ring is a white gold band with a line of small diamonds on top. My ring has small diamonds going all the way around. It looks beautiful with my engagement ring.

We walk around the table to sign the marriage certificate. The photographer and the wedding coordinator sign the certificate as our witnesses. We walk back to our spots and the notary walks out from behind the table. He stands so Rey and I are directly in front of him. We face each other.

"I now pronounce you man and wife. Rey, kiss your bride," The notary says.

Rey reaches for me. He kisses me passionately. I immediately feel the butterflies in my belly take flight. When our kiss breaks, we both start laughing. Everyone's cheering. We turn toward our four guests. Hugs and kisses erupt. Sasha, the wedding coordinator, appears a few minutes later with a tray of champagne glasses and makes a toast.

"I met the two of you yesterday, but your love is so infectious. Everyone wishes for love like yours. This is, by far, the smallest wedding I've ever planned but it's been the most romantic. You both only cared about marrying each other and everything else was just details. It warmed my heart more than you know." Her hand goes into the air with her glass. "To Rey and Kat, may you have much happiness and lots of love always." Everyone does the same and takes a sip. She gives the two of us a quick hug and heads to another wedding.

Lunch is served on the deck of our cottage. We arranged for a DJ to play right on the sand. The two-tiered cake sits a few feet away on a smaller table. It's white with little pearl accents all over it. We decide to have K & R as the cake topper in silver. Once we finish our meal, Rey and I cut the cake and have it for dessert.

Paul stands up and clears his throat. We look at him.

"Rey and Kat, we're so happy for you. I know this hasn't been a traditional wedding, but you need to dance for the first time as husband and wife." Paul signals to the DJ.

Rey grabs my hand and leads me to the sand just off the deck. The song 'Bless the Broken Road' by

Rascal Flatts starts to play. I bring my arms up around his neck and lean my cheek to his. His arms come around my waist and we hold each other tightly as we dance. I see the photographer snapping pictures from the corner of my eye and smile. I can't wait to see these pictures.

When the song ends, we kiss softly. I smile at him and go take my seat while Rey gets his mother. He places his hand out to her and she takes it. They start dancing to the song 'A Song for Mama by Boys II Men. Tears fall down Luisa's face. Rey wipes them away and kisses her cheek. Tears fall down my cheeks as I watch them. I think of my son. My heart hurts that my family isn't here to celebrate this amazing day with me. Rey must've sensed something because he looks up. I give him a small smile. He doesn't take his eyes off mine while he dances with his mother. As soon as the song ends, he comes over to me.

"What's wrong, baby?" he asks as he wipes the tears from my face.

"I was thinking of my family and how I'll never get to dance with my son," I say as the tears fell again. He brings me to him and holds me tightly.

"I know. I'm so sorry," he says and holds me. I get it out and pull away.

"I'm done. I just had a moment. I'm sorry".

"Never apologize for mourning your family." He kisses me with so much love. He smiles when our kiss breaks.

The six of us dance all afternoon. The photographer wants to get some shots of us on the beach as the sun's setting. Once all the pictures are taken, Luisa and Paul come to say their goodbyes.

"We've had a wonderful time," Luisa says. "We're going to head back to the room. We need to pack and get some rest. Our flight's early tomorrow morning." She looks at me and takes my hands. "We're so proud and honored to have you as a daughter-in-law. I love you, sweetheart." She pulls me to her, and I hug her tightly. Paul comes up, kisses my cheek, and hugs the two of us.

We pull apart and I look at both of them. "Thank you for coming out and for being so great. I love you both so very much. Have a safe trip back and we'll see you in a week."

They're hugging Rey when Uncle Manny and Aunt Lina come to say their goodbyes, as well. A few minutes later, the four of them head toward the main hotel.

Chapter 53

Kat

Rey takes my hand and kisses it. He leads me to the glass doors that lead into our cottage. He picks me up and carries me inside. He sets me down gently and leads me to the couch. We sit down, and Rey looks at me.

"I have something for you," he says, and I smile.

"What? Why?" I ask.

"It's just a little something." He reaches into his pocket and pulls out a small box. He hands it to me. I take it and look at him.

"You didn't need to get me anything."

"I know I didn't, but I needed to get you that."

I look down at the box and slowly open it. I look at it and back up at Rey. He smiles at me, and I look back at the box. It's a locket charm for my charm bracelet. It has R&K engraved on the outside. I pick it up and open the locket. Inside is a picture taken of us at Christmas on one side and the other side is empty.

"The empty side is for one of our wedding pictures. I already spoke to the photographer and told him we needed a small photo for a locket."

"I love it. It's beautiful. Can you put it on me?" I hand him the locket and my wrist. He puts it on and kisses my wrist. "I love you."

"I love you," he says. I take his hand and stand.

"It's time for your gift now." I pull him to his feet and lead him to the bedroom. When we step into the bedroom, I push him to sit on the bed. I remove his jacket and bend to remove his shoes. I take his jacket and shoes to the chair in the corner. I walk back to Rey and stop in front of him. I turn my back to him.

"Unzip me, please."

I feel his hand on the zipper of my dress. I bring my hands up to hold my dress in place once he unzips it. I feel the heat from his fingers grab the zipper and push it down. I step away from him as soon as I know the zipper is down. I'm standing in the middle of the room staring at him. He watches me intently. I turn so I'm facing him. I let the dress fall.

Rey's mouth drops open. I'm nervous but Rey's reaction almost makes me laugh. Almost. His eyes get dark as he looks at me. I feel his eyes rake over my body.

I'm wearing a white corset with a white lace thong. My right thigh has a light blue garter. I left my shoes on. I've never worn any type of lingerie in front of Rey but my normal bra and panties. I'm too shy and insecure about myself to think of buying stuff like this. I don't know if Rey likes it.

"Baby, you look stunning." He stands and makes his way over to me. He picks up my hand and turns me. When our eyes lock, he takes a deep breath. "You're the most beautiful woman I've ever laid eyes on. You were gorgeous all those years ago and age has done amazing things to your beauty. You're more gorgeous now than ever before."

I smile at him. "Do you like it?"

"Sweetheart, I love it. I can't take my eyes off you." His eyes travel down my body again.

"I feel so out of place. I've never worn anything like this before."

Rey brings his hands to my face and kisses me deeply. "Feel free to wear more of this. It's incredible and the best gift anyone has ever given me."

He kisses me again but this time he kisses me so passionately. I feel like I'm going to explode from the heat of it. We're always extremely heated for each other but tonight our passion's igniting. He breaks the kiss and looks at me. There's a fire in his eyes.

"I have been dying to make love to my wife." I nearly melt on the spot.

"I never thought I would ever hear those words from your mouth."

"I never thought I'd be saying them to you." I move my hands to his shirt and start undoing the buttons. His lips find my neck and chest. I shove the shirt off his shoulders and let it drop to the floor. I unbuckle his belt and remove it. He quickly pushes his pants down and takes his socks along with them. I look over his body and shutter. He kisses me again. As we kiss, we move back toward the bed. When the back of my knees hit the bed, I break the kiss to climb on the bed. He follows and lies next to me.

His hands touch every part of me as my hands do the same. The feeling of his hard muscles is driving me crazy. He always does this to me. I can't get enough of him. Rey must've sensed my urgency because he nods.

"I know. Me too, but I also don't want to rush this," he whispers. "Sit up, baby." I sit up and he goes to work removing the corset. Once the last latch releases, he slowly pulls it away from my body, and my breasts spill out. He takes a deep breath and growls. "You're beautiful."

He dips his head toward my breasts and feasts on them. I'm completely lost in the feelings. He always makes me feel so cherished. I hope I do the same for him. He pushes me gently back onto the bed.

His fingers come to the waistband of my thong, and I lift my hips. He pushes my thong off my hips, down my legs, and off in one move. He quickly removes his boxers and comes to lie on top of me. His hands rest on either side of my head and he props on his elbows.

"I want to take this slow, baby, but I can't take it anymore. I need you now."

"Me too, love." I close my eyes and revel in the sensations his body is bringing out of me.

"Open your eyes. I want to see every emotion. I want us to watch each other," he says. I nod, and our lips collide. He kisses me like he never has before and I'm breathless when he pulls away. He enters me and we moan.

"Oh god! You feel so good!" I gasp.

"I feel like I'm in heaven."

He starts moving and I match him thrust for thrust. We never break eye contact and, within a few minutes, we're coming together. I shatter and let out a scream. Rey groans loudly.

"I love you so much," he says as he comes. He collapses on top of me, and I love the feel of his weight. I've never felt so safe.

"I love you," I breathe. He lifts his head and smiles. His mouth comes down on mine and we kiss. That night, we went out to the beach and made love on the sand. We came in and made love again in the shower. We spent the night wrapped up in each other and our love. It was a perfect wedding night.

Chapter 54

Kat

A week later, Rey carries me over the threshold of our house. As we come through the door, Champ's at our heels. He's climbing up Rey's leg. Rey sets me down and laughs.

"Ok, little buddy." He picks him up. Champ licks all over Rey's hands. I laugh and scratch behind his little ears. He closes his eyes in complete bliss. Rey laughs. "It feels good, huh?"

We continue to give Champ some love when Katie comes from the bathroom. Katie is our neighbor. Katie and her husband Sam live two houses down and we became friends shortly after we moved in. She's pregnant and due to give birth any minute now. We were going to kennel Champ, but she said she would watch him. She insisted she would love to do something since she couldn't do anything else. She would come and spend some time with Champ every day and feed him. She also brought in the mail for us and kept an eye on the house.

"Hey, guys!" she says as she approaches us.

"Hi!" I give her a small hug. "How are you feeling?"

"I haven't been feeling too good today. My back's killing me, and the pain seems to be getting worse," Katie says.

I look at Rey and he doesn't seem to think anything of it. I look back at Katie.

"How long have you been experiencing the pain?" I ask.

"It started about two hours ago."

"Does the pain persist, or does it come and go?"

"It comes and goes." She doesn't seem to get where I'm going with the questioning. I see the panic come across her face as she realizes it.

"Katie, honey, take a deep breath. How's the pain now?"

"It's okay, but I feel another spasm coming," she says.

"Can I feel your belly?" I ask, and she nods her head. I place my hands on her belly and it's rock hard. I look up at Rey.

"Rey, please back the car out of the garage and call Sam. Tell him we're taking Katie to the hospital. She's in labor," I tell him. He runs, puts Champ in his kennel, and into the garage, taking his cell phone out of his pocket. Katie leans against the wall and closes her eyes.

"Breath sweetie," I tell her and look at my watch. When the pain seems to subside, I grab her arm and lead her to the car. I help get her into the passenger seat. I quickly run back into the house and grab our coats and my purse. I lock up and run back to the car. "Katie, where's your suitcase?"

"It's in Sam's car." She's hunched over a little, taking deep breaths. I look at my watch again. The contractions are only five minutes apart.

"You're doing great, Katie. Breathe through them," I tell her.

"I just spoke to Sam and he's on his way to the hospital," Rey says as I jump into the backseat. When I'm safely in, he takes off.

****

Two hours later, Rey and I sit in the hospital waiting room. Sam came out once to update us, but he hasn't been out in over an hour. I look at Rey as he flips through a magazine.

"Are you okay?" I ask him. He seems so panicked.

"Yes. I'm just nervous. I hope everything's okay in there," he says but doesn't look up at me. I touch his arm and he finally looks at me. He gives me a weak smile. "A part of me is a little glad we can't have children."

"Why?" I ask, really confused now.

"I don't think I could bear seeing you in that much pain and not being able to do anything about it." I smile at him. My heart swells at the sentiment.

"I understand. I felt the same way when I saw you in a hospital bed and I couldn't do anything to make it better. Then, I had to watch you go through the pain of physical therapy. It killed me to watch it. I felt so helpless," I tell him.

He turns in his seat to face me. "You being there for me is how I got through it. The pain was rough. You made it better by supporting me and loving me."

I see Sam come through the double doors. I quickly stand, and Rey does the same. We walk over to Sam, and he has the biggest smile on his face.

"My son has arrived!" Sam says. Rey and I jump and hug him.

"Congratulations, Sam!" Rey shakes his hand.

"Congratulations! How's Katie?" I ask.

"Katie and the baby are doing wonderful!"

We hug him again and he runs back in. He told us he would come to get us in a few minutes so we could see Katie and the baby.

I look at Rey and he opens his arms to me. I walk into them and hug him tightly. So many emotions are running through me. I'm trying, with all my might, not to cry. We stand like this for a long time. When Sam comes to get us, we're still in our embrace.

"Are you ready to come in?" Sam asks us.

"Yes." Rey and I say in unison. We laugh and follow Sam to Katie's room.

When we walk into the room, I see Katie holding the baby. I stop at the sink to wash my hands. Rey follows my lead and washes his hands as well. I go to Katie and look at the beautiful little boy in her arms. I lean down, hug her, and congratulate her. Rey looks at him over my shoulder. I step away and Rey hugs Katie.

"Kat, would you like to hold him?" Katie asks, and I nod.

"I would love to." I step toward her to take the baby from her. I walk him toward the window and look at his little face. He's so perfect. "Do you have a name?"

"Logan Samuel," Katie says with a big smile.

"A strong name for a strong boy." I continue rocking him. I can't hold back my tears any longer. They fall on my face like waterfalls. Memories of holding my babies when they were born and memories of holding them when they died flood my brain. My heart breaks all over again and I pray this perfect little boy will live a long happy life and Katie will never feel the kind of pain I feel every single day.

Rey comes up to me and places his hands on my shoulders. That simple touch gives me so much strength. I take a deep breath and instantly calm. I wipe my face. I turn to return Logan to Katie when I see them staring at me. They have stunned expressions on their faces.

I smile at them and hand Logan to Katie.

"He's beautiful. I'm so happy for you both." Sam comes to stand next to Katie and they smile at me. I feel Rey standing behind me and take a deep breath. "I need to explain what that was all about."

"You don't have to," Sam says.

"Yes, I do." I turn and look at Rey. He comes up beside me and takes my hand. I look back at Sam and Katie. "I lost my two kids six years ago in a car accident." They both gasp and Katie brings her hand to her mouth. "In the same car accident, I also lost my husband and my parents. It was a huge blow. Today was the first time I held a child since my kids passed." Tears fall down Katie's cheeks and Sam comes to me. I see the tears falling down his cheeks. He pulls me to him and hugs me tightly.

"I'm so sorry, Kat. I can't even imagine what you're feeling." Sam pulls away from me. He looks at Rey and I can tell he doesn't know what else to say.

"Thank you, Sam." I kiss Katie's cheek. "Congratulations again. Enjoy every moment with him." I smile at her. She nods as I turn and walk out of the room. I need a moment to get my emotions in check.

Chapter 55

I watch as Kat walks out of the room. I know she needs a minute alone. Katie's crying quietly, looking down at the baby. Sam's wiping his face. He looks at me.

"Is she going to be okay?" Sam asks.

"Kat's the strongest person I know. She's gone through so much and seems to come out on the other side every single time. I don't know if I could've survived something like that. I can't imagine losing a child, let alone both on the same day." I tell them. Sam nods in agreement. "She just needs some time alone, so I'm giving it to her."

"I have a new respect for Kat," Katie whispers. She looks down at the baby in her arms. "My heart hurts for her."

"Please don't feel sorry for her. She hates that. She doesn't like it when people dwell on it or keep reminding her of it. She told you because you guys are good friends and we're going to watch that beautiful little man grow up. She knows she'll get emotional at times, and she wanted you to know why."

"Maybe you can have a child to fill a little of the void," Sam says, and I shake my head.

"She can't have any more children. Her uterus was punctured in the car accident, and she had to have an emergency hysterectomy." Sam runs a hand through his hair and closes his eyes.

"Geez, the poor girl can't catch a break." He mutters.

"I better go check on her." I extend my hand to Sam. He takes it and we shake. I congratulate him again and walk over to Katie. I kiss the top of her head and kiss Logan's forehead. I congratulate her as well and say my goodbyes.

I head out of the hospital room and find Kat on the floor just outside the room. She has her chin resting on her knees and her arms around her legs. She stares straight ahead. I don't think she knows I'm there. I squat down and place my hand on her arm. She jumps, and her head snaps up to me.

"It's me, baby," I say, and she gives me a small smile.

"I'm sorry," she says.

"You don't have anything to apologize for." She starts to get up and I reach out to help her. She grabs my hand.

"Can we go home?" She asks.

"Of course." We head out of the hospital. As I walk her to the car, I look at her. She seems so lost. I wish I could take it all away from her. "Is there anything I can do for you?" She stops walking and turns to me.

"You're doing it. You let me grieve and don't tell me I should be over it. You understand I need to do this sometimes. You understand I'll always grieve for my family. You love me and that's all I need," I nod, and we continue walking.

A few minutes later, we're in the car and on our way home.

****

When we get home, Kat goes into our bedroom and straight to the bathroom. She turns on the shower and walks into her closet. She removes her clothes and steps into the shower. She turns and looks at me.

"Join me, please." I nod. I quickly undress and step in behind her. Her back is to me and her face is facing the spray. She stands there and lets the water fall down her face. I don't move and watch her. I pray she doesn't fall into a deep depression again.

I step toward her and pick up the washcloth. I soap it up and begin to wash her. She opens her eyes and looks at me. I finish washing her body and grab the shampoo. I put some in my hand and start to shampoo her hair. She closes her eyes as I massage her head. I place her head under the spray and remove the shampoo from her hair. I apply the conditioner to her hair and comb the knots out. I rinse it out. I turn on the second showerhead and proceed to wash up quickly. When I'm done, I turn both showers off. I grab a towel and dry off Kat. I wrap it around her while I dry off. I run a towel through her hair to dry it as best I can.

I pick her up and take her to bed. I lie her down and she curls to her side. I climb in behind her and spoon her. I hold her until I hear her breathing even out and I know she's asleep.

Chapter 56

Kat

Three months have passed since Logan was born. We've become closer to Katie and Sam. Katie didn't know anything about babies, so I help her as much as I can. Their immediate family is far, and they don't have any help. Katie and I have become good friends. I'm happy to have a friend again.

It's Saturday night and Rey and I decide to do a game night. We invite Rey's parents along with Sam and Katie. I'm in the kitchen finishing the dinner prep when Luisa comes in. I hug her.

"Can I help with anything?" Luisa asks.

"No, thanks. Have a seat." I pull out a stool from the kitchen island and hand her a glass of wine.

"You spoil me." She takes a sip of the wine. We start laughing when Rey, Paul, Sam, and Katie come in. Sam carries little Logan in his carrier. I smile when I see them. Hugs are exchanged, and Sam puts Logan down in a corner. He's fast asleep. The champ goes over and sniffs him. He lies down next to Logan and falls asleep. He's so protective of the baby. He's such a sweet puppy.

Dinner is served and we dig in. We talk, eat, and enjoy each other's company. I'm having such a good time. I squeeze Rey's hand under the table, and he smiles at me. I've never been happier. Rey and his family are amazing, and I can't imagine my life without them.

"Who's ready for dessert?" I ask as I stand. I see smiles all around and Paul grunts.

"Girl, you put me in a food coma every time we have dinner here," Paul says as I laugh.

"Are you sure, Paul? I made your favorite." I start to clear the plates. I look back at Paul and his eyes light up.

"You made apple pie?"

"Yes, I did," I say, smiling at him.

"Homemade apple pie?" Sam asks. Paul looks over at him.

"Yes. She makes the most amazing apple pie." Paul and Sam rub their hands together. The table erupts with laughter, and I walk into the kitchen with the dirty dishes.

****

We finish the first game when Logan starts to fuss. Katie gets up and starts to make him a bottle. Sam picks him up out of the carrier. He's such a great baby. Sam brings him over to us and he's all smiles. Luisa asks to hold him and takes him from Sam. She showers him in kisses until Katie comes back into the room. Logan looks around the room and his little eyes land on me.

"Hi there, beautiful boy," I say, and he gives me the biggest smile. He starts pushing his little body toward me. Everyone's watching. I put my hands out and he pushes more until he reaches my hands. I take him from Luisa, and he places his little head on my shoulder. My heart swells. I look at Katie and see the tears swell in her eyes. I look away quickly before I start to cry. Katie comes to me and shows Logan the bottle. He looks at it and picks his head up. Katie places her hands out, so she can take him. He moves toward her but pulls back and looks at me. He gives me a big smile and places his little head on my shoulder again.

"It looks like he wants Aunt Kat to feed him," she says as she hands me the bottle. I turn him, lay him on my lap, and place the bottle in his mouth. He starts sucking on it. I look up and Rey's watching me. He smiles at me and mouths 'I love you. I watch as Logan devours his bottle. I put him back up to my shoulder and burp him. Once he burps, he places his head on my shoulder and falls back to sleep.

"You have the magic touch, Kat," Katie says. "I swear he has a big crush on you."

Everyone laughs.

"Rey and Kat, Katie, and I would like to ask you something," Sam says as he stands. He goes to Katie and places his hands on her shoulders.

I look at him and give him my undivided attention. "Sure, Sam. Ask away." Rey says.

Katie smiles up at Sam and they look back at us.

"Would you be Logan's godparents?" Sam asks. I immediately feel the tears swell in my eyes. I rub Logan's back and try to blink the tears away. I look at Rey and he has a huge smile on his face. He looks at me and nods. I nod back at him.

"We would be honored." Rey stands. He shakes Sam's hand and gives Katie a big hug. I stand slowly and hug them. Paul and Luisa are watching and smiling. Katie looks at me. I'm still trying to fight the tears.

"Kat, you've been an unbelievable friend for the last couple of months. You've done more for me than my own family and I can't thank you enough. You're amazing with Logan and he's totally in love with you. Logan's a lucky little boy to have you and Rey as his godparents. I've never seen two people, who aren't his parents, give a little boy so much love. We're the ones who are honored to have you as godparents to our son. We love you both," Katie says.

"I love this little boy so much and it means the world to me you asked us to be his godparents," I tell her. I can't fight the tears anymore and they fall down my cheeks.

"I can tell you were an amazing mom. I know Logan's the only baby you've been around since you lost yours. I know how hard this is for you, but I also know Logan has healed you somehow," she says. I nod and see her tears.

"He's a little angel. My kids sent him to me. I'll always protect him and care for him. Anytime you or he needs me, I'll be there," I tell them.

I walk Logan to his carrier and gently place him in. I buckle him in as Katie and Sam announce they're going to head home. We say our goodbyes and they leave.

Rey and I walk back into the kitchen and Paul's clearing the table. Luisa's loading the dessert dishes into the dishwasher.

"Luisa, leave that. I'll take care of it," I say as she turns to me.

She waves me off. "I only have a few more pieces," and continues loading.

I go to Paul and take the pie and coffee out of his hands. I put them on the counter and start wrapping up the apple pie when Paul places his hand on mine. I look up at him.

"Sam and Katie couldn't have picked better godparents," he whispers.

"Thank you, Paul. It means the world to me if you think that," I say and look down.

Rey hugs me from behind.

"Are you okay?" he asks in my ear.

"I am. Logan's an angel sent to me by my babies. The tears I shed and will shed are of contentment. I know they're happy and they're letting me know it through Logan," I tell him and turn in his arm. I kiss him softly.

I turn back around and look at the three of them. These three people are my whole world. I'm so happy. I smile at them. "I love all of you."

The smile that spreads across their faces says everything I need. Everything's okay. I'm okay. My guardian angels sent them to me. They made sure I'm surrounded by love. My heart's finally full again.

The End

SONGS MENTIONED IN THE BOOK

'Wanted' by Hunter Hayes

'Open Arms' by Journey

'Save the Last Dance for Me by Michael Bublé

'Masterpiece' by Atlantic Starr

'Bless the Broken Road' by Rascal Flatts

'A Song for Mama' by Boys II Men

Made in the USA
Columbia, SC
30 January 2024

30760702R00173